HER CYBORG BEAST

INTERSTELLAR BRIDES® PROGRAM: THE
COLONY - 4

GRACE GOODWIN

Published by KSA Publishers
Goodwin, Grace
Her Cyborg Beast, Interstellar Brides® Program: The Colony - 4

Publisher's Note:
This book was written for an adult audience. The book may contain explicit
sexual content. Sexual activities included in this book are strictly fantasies
intended for adults and any activities or risks taken by fictional characters
within the story are neither endorsed nor encouraged by the author or
publisher.

GET A FREE BOOK!

INTERSTELLAR BRIDES® PROGRAM

YOUR mate is out there. Take the test today and discover your perfect match. Are you ready for a sexy alien mate (or two)?

VOLUNTEER NOW!
interstellarbridesprogram.com

1

J, Interstellar Bride Processing Center, Miami, Florida

"I STAND. NO BED." A DEEP, RUMBLING VOICE FILLED MY HEAD. My mind. My body. This body knew that voice. Knew it and shivered in anticipation. Somehow I knew this male was mine. He was huge. Not in his normal state. He had some kind of sickness. A fever that would cause him to go insane if I didn't tame him. Fuck him. Make him mine forever.

I felt the softness of a bed at my back—my *naked* back—and then I was hoisted up as if I weighed nothing. That was a joke because I weighed plenty. I wasn't a tiny waif or a Victoria's Secret model. Well, I was tall like one, just over six feet, but I had boobs and hips. Strong hands banded about my waist, spun me about so my back was pressed to his front. His *naked* front. Hands slid up and cupped my breasts.

Oh.

Wow.

Um.

Yes. God, yes.

This was crazy. Completely crazy. I didn't like to be manhandled. Hell, I did the manhandling. I ate weak men for breakfast and made stronger ones cry by lunchtime. All in a day's work.

But I wasn't at work now.

I had no idea where the hell I was, but this guy knew just how to push every one of my hot buttons. Or should I say, *her* hot buttons. I wasn't me. Well, I was here, but this wasn't me. The thoughts going through my head, the knowledge, wasn't mine. But the reactions? One tug on my nipples and my pussy was wet and aching. Empty.

I felt the hot throb of his cock against my back. He was tall, really tall based on how far down the bed was from me now. Yet his hands cupped all of my breasts. They usually were overflowing. Triple Ds tended to do that, but not with him. Nope.

I felt…small.

But, this wasn't me. Was it?

It *felt* like me.

"Better," he growled, walking us both slowly toward a table. We were in some kind of room, sterile and impersonal, like a hotel room with a big bed, table and chairs. I couldn't see much else, but I wasn't looking because as soon as my thighs bumped into the cool edge of the table, he leaned forward, forcing me down over the top. I resisted. "Down, mate."

Mate?

I bristled at the firm hand pushing me down, at his commanding tone. That word. I wasn't anyone's mate. I didn't date. I fucked, sure, but I was the one to walk away. I was the one on top, in control. But now? I had zero control, and it was uncomfortable. But the need to let go, to let this guy take over? I wanted it. Well, my pussy did. My nipples did, too. And the woman whose body I inhabited, she wanted it, too. But unlike me, she wasn't afraid. She didn't fight this, or him.

She resisted because she knew he wanted her to. Knew it would make his cock hard and his pulse race. Knew it would push him to the edge of control. She wanted to make sure that when it came to control, she had none. The thought of the cuffs—cuffs?—she knew were coming made her pussy clench with heat.

Which was just damn weird to me, but there was nothing I could do about it. I was a witness and participant, but I wasn't really here. I felt like a ghost inside her body, living someone else's fantasy.

Hot fantasy, sure. But not real. This wasn't real.

This body was all about letting the big brute do anything he wanted. My mind had other ideas. But I had no control here. This body wasn't mine. The thoughts going through my head weren't mine either. This woman— me—whoever I was right now—wanted to push him. She wanted to be dominated. She wanted to be conquered. Controlled. Fucked until she screamed. And I was simply along for the ride. "I don't like to be bossed around," she/I said.

"Liar." I saw a big hand settle onto the table beside me, saw the blunt fingers, the scars, the dusting of hair on the wrist. Felt the other big hand pressing into my back. Harder. More insistent.

I hissed when my breasts came in contact with the hard surface, and I put my elbows out to keep from being lowered all the way, but he changed tactics, his hand moving from my back to my pussy, two fingers sliding deep. "Wet. Mine."

I felt the broad expanse of his torso against my back, his skin hot, the hard length of his cock rubbing along my wet slit, teasing. And he was right. I was wet. Hot. So eager for

3

him I was afraid this crazy woman—whose body I currently inhabited—was going to break down and *beg*. *Beg!*

His lips brushed along my spine, fingers slid my hair to the side, and his kisses continued along my neck as his hands worked their magic. One pressing me slowly, inevitably toward a prone position on the table. The other rubbed my bare bottom, huge fingers dipping toward my core, sliding deep, retreating to stroke my sensitive bottom again in a repetitive tease that made me squirm.

The gesture was gentle, reverent even, and completely at odds with his dominance. Two metal bracelets came into my view as he set them down in front of me. Silver toned, they were thick and wide, with decorative etchings in them.

The sight made me hotter, the woman's reaction nearly orgasmic. She wanted them on her wrists, heavy and permanent. They would mark her as his mate. Forever.

I had no idea where they came from, but my mind wasn't working properly, and I couldn't figure it out. Not with the soft lips, the flick of his tongue, the prodding of his cock over my slick folds and the rush of longing filling me.

The bracelets looked old and matched ones that were already on his wrists. I hadn't noticed them before now, but that didn't surprise me.

He shifted, opening one and putting it on my wrist, then the other. Even though I was pressed into the table by his formidable body, I didn't feel threatened. It felt like he was giving me a gift of some kind, something precious.

I just had no idea what.

"They're beautiful," I heard myself say.

He growled again, the rumbling of it vibrating from his chest and into my back. "Mine. Bad girl. Fuck now."

I had no idea why I'd be a bad girl, especially if his cock was as big as it felt. I wanted it.

"Yes. Do it!" I spread my legs wider, not sure what he

expected, but knowing I didn't care. I wanted him to fuck me now. I didn't want to be good. I wanted to be bad. Very, very bad.

Evidently, I'd lost my mind because I had no idea what he looked like. Who he was. Where I was. But none of that mattered. And why did the idea of being manhandled or even spanked appeal like it never had before?

He shifted his hips, slid his cock over my folds, and it settled at my entrance. I felt the broad head, so big that it parted my slick lips, and as he pressed in, I whimpered.

He was huge. Like enormous. He was careful as he filled me, as if he knew he might be too much.

I shifted my hips, tried to take him, but my inner walls clenched and squeezed, tried to adjust. My hands couldn't find purchase on the smooth surface, and I lowered myself down, put my cheek against the wood, angling my hips up.

He slid in a touch farther.

I gasped, shook my head. "Too big." My voice was soft, breathy. He wasn't. He'd fit. He might hurt me, might shock me, but I wanted him. Every damn inch.

"Shh," he crooned.

From nowhere, a memory surfaced of this male speaking to me when I'd been worried about this moment. His beast— what was a beast?—*You can take a beast's cock. You were made for it. You were made for me.*

As he slid in to the hilt and I felt his hips press against my bottom, I had to agree with him. I was milking him and clenching down, adjusting to being filled so much, but it felt good.

God, did it ever.

"Ready, mate?"

Ready? For what? He was already in.

But when he pulled back all the way so my folds clung to him before he plunged deep, I realized I hadn't been ready.

The pounding stole the breath from my lungs, but I almost came. I had no idea how because I'd never come from just vaginal penetration only. I needed to rub my clit with my own fingers.

When he did it again, I realized fingers were definitely not needed.

"Yes!" I cried. I couldn't help it. I wanted it. Needed it. I shimmied, pressed back as he plunged in once more.

His hand moved, gripped my wrists, held onto the bracelets.

He held me down and fucked me.

There was no escape. No reprieve. No stopping him as the orgasm built into a dangerous thing. And I wanted all of it. I wanted *him*.

"Come. Now. Scream. I fill you up."

He was a dirty talker, too. Not much for complete sentences, but that was part of his charm.

I was so drenched for him I could hear the wet slap of our bodies as he pounded into me. I could feel the wet coating in the cool air, slipping from me and down my thighs.

Holding me down with one hand, he grabbed my bottom with the other, a full lobe in his grasp, pulling me open. Wider.

He pushed deeper. Harder. I thrashed on the table, both excited and vulnerable, stretched out before him. Unable to move. Unable to resist. I had to accept whatever he wanted to give me. Trust. Surrender.

The thought made me groan, my body spiraling ever higher as I fought, holding back my final fall.

He released my bottom, a single sharp spank landing like liquid heat on my bare skin. And that orgasm he commanded from me? The one I was holding back? Yeah, there it was. I screamed, arched my back, my hard nipples chafing against the table top as I lost control, went blind, an abyss opening up to swallow me as I shattered.

I lost all sense of myself, my only reality the hard thrust of his cock as he pumped into me as my pussy milked him.

"Mate," he said, just before he sank deep, settled, then roared like an animal.

It was like a beast had filled him, taken over. Claimed me.

I felt his seed, hot and thick, coating me deep inside. It was too much for me to hold as he moved again, fucking me through his release, his hot seed sliding from me and down my thighs.

I felt so good and so wrong. Controlled. Overpowered. Blatantly claimed.

Bad. Bad. Bad. I was soooo bad right now.

I didn't even try to get up, not even when he released my wrists and grabbed my hips to pull me back. Hard. He lifted my ass off the table and pulled me onto his cock which was already swelling. Ready for more.

I groaned, trying to move my arms. No luck, but something rattled. The sound odd. Out of place.

"Stay." He grunted the order and thrust into me again. Submitting to him went against everything I was, and yet... my pussy clenched with his barked command. Perhaps I wasn't everything I imagined.

His fingers dug deep, pulling me back until he bottomed out inside me.

Yes!

I was hot all over again. Ready for more. Needy. I could go for hours...

"Caroline." The voice came from out of nowhere. Cold. Clinical. A woman's voice.

Who?

Everything faded even as I struggled to stay in that body,

as he pulled out and slowly filled me again. Spread me open. I groaned, fighting for it. Fighting to stay with him.

"Caroline!" Sharp this time. Insistent. Like a teacher scolding her student.

Oh God. The testing...

I gasped—this time not from pleasure—and my eyes flew open.

Instead of bracelets about my wrists, I had restraints. I was naked, but I wasn't bent over with my lover's hands on my hips. I was shackled to a medical exam chair wearing an Interstellar Brides Processing Center gown. The logo tracked up and down the hospital-style gown in neat, perfect rows of burgundy on gray fabric.

Clinical. Sterile. All business.

I wasn't pressed over a hard table. I wasn't being filled and fucked until my entire body exploded. There was no giant man.

There was only me and a stern looking woman in her late twenties. Gray eyes. Dark brown hair coiled tightly into a bun at the base of her skull. She looked like a grumpy ballerina, and her name floated to the surface even before I read her name tag.

Warden Egara. She was doing my testing. Testing for the Interstellar Brides Program. A process which would match me to an alien and send me into outer space to be his wife.

Forever.

arlord Rezzer, The Colony, Base 3, Medical Station

HAD THIS BEEN A NORMAL DAY, EVEN THE TWO HULKING Prillon warriors holding me down would not have been able to stop me.

Today was not normal. I hadn't been normal since I'd gone into that cave after Krael and the Hive Integration Units.

Maxim and Ryston each held a shoulder in place as I growled at the doctor. "What do you mean my beast is gone forever?"

I scowled at Doctor Surnen and waited for an explanation, despite the fact that I knew it was not coming.

"I can't explain it, Warlord. Whatever the Hive did to you, I can't undo."

Behind him, Maxim's and Ryston's mate, a human woman named Rachel, stared at me with big, sad eyes; a sorrowful gaze I couldn't stand to meet. "We'll figure it out, Rezz. I promise you, I *will* figure it out."

Rachel was a brilliant scientist, and she'd already saved Maxim and several others from Hive threats.

However, every one of my limbs felt weak. Empty. Each day that passed, I became more convinced that it was too late for me.

Maxim and Ryston were holding me back. Not just because I was angry, but because their beautiful mate was so close. I had not lost my honor with my beast. I would not harm a hair on her head. To do that I would have to be enraged. To hurt anyone in this room, I would need to go beast. Go into a rage, or the mating fever. Somehow, the Hive had stolen that from me, and I was only angry.

I was weak now. Not Atlan, because a true Atlan male had an inner beast. I didn't any longer. No beast. Nothing.

Ignoring Rachel's promise completely, I turned back to the doctor. Promises had no place in my life, not on this world, because I was resigned to a life here—on The Colony —with the other contaminated warriors. "Has this ever happened before? To another Atlan?"

The doctor scanned his tablet again. A worried frown marred his brow. Doctor Surnen had seen more death and destruction than I wanted to know about. He served with us, the contaminated, because he, too, was not allowed to return to his home world, to Prillon Prime. His left hand had been completely transformed. Cyborg. Alien. Hive.

My job had been to rip the Hive to shreds. I did not repair the damage they inflicted. I survived it. The Cyborg implants in my body made it impossible for me to return to my home planet of Atlan, and now it would seem the core of who and what I was had also been stolen from me.

Maxim cursed. "You never should have gone down into

those caves after that fucker Krael. We should have called in the Fleet."

Ryston's grip on my arm tightened as he argued with the governor "We *are* the Coalition. Just because we're cyborg does not mean we're less. We can't start thinking like that. The Hive are here, in our backyard, and we need to take care of it."

Rachel was pacing, her hands going to her thick hair. She rubbed her temples as if she were agitated. As if her head hurt from thinking too hard. "I just don't understand what they're trying to accomplish. When they took you, why not a hand like Doctor Surnen or even an arm? Why steal your beast? And how the hell did they do it? What possible good can it do them?"

Maxim shook his head. "I don't know, mate, but we will figure it out." He looked to me with his usual sharp gaze. "Listen to me, Rezz. You can't give up the fight."

I leaned back in the exam chair. Not because they were holding me back, but because I didn't care enough to argue. Truth was truth. I could feel it along with the strange sense of apathy that took the place of what was missing. A vital part of me.

The Hive had taken my beast.

The one thing that made me who and what I was. A Warlord, a beast among men, frightening on the battlefield. Powerful enough to face any obstacle, to protect a female, to be worthy of the title, Warlord. And now I felt nothing when I should be feeling rage. I should have turned. Grown. Changed into the beast. Ripped the med unit to pieces.

But no. I was numb. Cold. Dead. That was my new existence. When I looked at Rachel, I did not see a beautiful woman. Not anymore. It was as if when they took my beast, they took everything that made me feel alive. I could look now at the curve of her breast, the soft skin of her face and feel...nothing. Not even envy for the two Prillon warriors who had put the copper colored collar around her neck and made her theirs.

The doctor turned away from us, his dark green uniform stretched across his large shoulders. He was a Prillon warrior as well, unmated and alone, like most inhabitants of The Colony. A few brides had begun to come to The Colony, and for the last few months, I had seen Rachel and Kristin grow heavy with child. Seen the happiness and contentment on my fellow warriors' faces.

With the brides' arrivals, I had thought, perhaps, my life could be different. Since I might no longer be a fighter out amongst the stars, I could be a mate. But I was wrong. The Hive had taken even that hope from me.

The doctor turned to Maxim and their eyes met. A slight nod from the governor was my only warning before thick, heavy manacles crept out from the table and locked me in place. Not just on my wrists and ankles, they sealed around my waist and my thighs as well. All the while Maxim and Ryston continued to hold me down. They weren't taking any chances. Had my beast been free to rage at them, even this would not have held me. As it was, the two Prillon warriors were more than strong enough to restrain me.

"What the fuck are you doing, Doctor?" I glanced at Rachel who was biting her lip, looking concerned. "What the fuck are you doing to me? Talk to me now."

Rachel took a step closer and stood at the base of the exam chair. She looked me in the eye when none of the warriors would. A fact which I would neither forget nor forgive them for later.

"Listen, Rezz, there's one thing we haven't tried. One thing we think might work to bring your beast back, to heal you."

I blinked slowly. Not a flicker of hope sprung to life with

her words. I was past hope. We'd been playing this game for weeks. Injections. Tests. Communication with the Coalition Fleet and the Intelligence Core. Even conversations with doctors on Atlan. No one had seen this before. I was the first, and only. I stared at Maxim's and Ryston's mate, at the pleading in her eyes and felt a cold trickle of dread snake down my spine. "What are you doing to me?"

Rachel reached out to put her hand on my leg, but Maxim's angry snarl caused her to remove it immediately. Before the Hive had stolen the soul right out of me, I would have appreciated the gesture, even been amused by Maxim's protective instincts. Now, I felt nothing. Without the beast within, I felt empty. Hollow.

The doctor pushed some buttons, made adjustments to his controls along the far wall. I didn't know what the fuck he was doing. I wasn't a doctor. I was a Warlord. I hunted the Hive. I killed them. I protected. I raged. That's what I did. That's what I knew. So when he rejoined Rachel with a slight sheen of sweat covering his brow, I knew whatever he was about to tell me wasn't going to be good. In fact, if I hadn't known better, I would have believed the doctor was afraid of what my reaction might be.

The doctor nodded at Ryston this time, and before I knew it, Ryston attached something to my head. Something I did not want.

I looked the doctor in the eye. He held my gaze, refusing to look away, refusing to back down. "The Interstellar Brides Program testing. It's the only thing we haven't tried, Rezz."

Rachel moved forward but stepped back again after a quick glance at Maxim. The look she flashed him her only apology for forgetting that he didn't want her touching me. I didn't blame him. I was broken. No female should want to touch me. Which was why this was a ludicrous idea. Rachel cleared her throat and crossed her arms. Trying to look stubborn. "Your beast is strong, Rezz. All you need to do is wake him up. Revive him. He'll come back to life if your mate arrives. He'll come. He'll come for her. He'll break through whatever the Hive did to you."

She seemed to believe her words, but she had no proof. No reason to say it except to make me feel better. Such faith was painful. Shame rushed through me, but at least I felt *something.* I closed my eyes to hide my reaction from her.

She wanted me to have a mate.

No. I was no longer worthy.

I could not go beast. I could not claim a female properly like a true Atlan. "Summoning a female for me is not acceptable. You can put me through the testing since you've got me strapped down." I glanced up at Ryston and Maxim with a harsh glare. "But I will refuse the match."

"You refuse to accept your mate?" the doctor asked.

I gritted my teeth and opened my eyes so he could see the rage building, the rage I could not express, the rage of an Atlan who had been stripped of everything he was. "I refuse the match. Look at me. I am not worthy of a female. I cannot protect her. I cannot claim her. This is wrong."

"You would rather die?" he asked. "Because right now, execution is your only other option. Unless you want me to ship you off to the Intelligence Core and let their scientists run experiments on you. You can't return to Atlan. You can't return to battle. And we can't allow you to remain—"

"Like this," I finished, my soul withering, turning black as, with each word, my feeling of helplessness grew. "Do you think I do not know what my options are?" I asked. "I am not fit to be a mate. I am not fit to serve the Fleet. I should be put down. Send me to the containment cells on Atlan and let it be done."

"No!" Rachel protested. She lay her palm flat just above my knee and ignored Maxim when he growled. "You can't give up. Worse, you can't let them beat you. They had you and you escaped. Survived. Just try. Try it. Get tested. Accept the testing results. Meet her. Talk to her. If you can't claim her, if you don't want her, she'll be matched to another. Someone else on The Colony. There's nothing to lose and everything to gain, Rezz. Please."

The numbness in me spread, but I saw logic in her argument. I was worthless as a warrior. Worthless as a mate. But I could do one good deed. I could bring a bride to The Colony so that another worthy male could find happiness.

I looked at the doctor. "Do it then. Now. Before I change my mind."

Rachel leaped back and practically raced to the control panel. The wires and gadgets on my head began to emit a strange humming energy. It was hypnotic, and I did not fight the trancelike state as I succumbed to the pull of what seemed like a dream.

It could have been a few minutes or a few hours. I had no way of knowing, and I did not remember what occurred. But when my eyes flickered open, all four stood looking down at me, and even Maxim had a smile on his face.

It was Rachel who could not contain her excitement. She was laughing and rocking back and forth, her big belly, which was swollen with her child from Ryston and Maxim, almost bumping the testing chair. "We found her, Rezz! You've been matched. And she's human. She's on her way now."

"Human?" I asked.

"Yes! From Earth. Like the rest of us. I can't wait to meet her."

The rest of us were the other females from the Brides Program who'd been matched to members of The Colony. It seemed all of us had a strong desire for Earthlings.

I glanced at the Prillon warriors surrounding me—

Maxim, Ryston and Doctor Surnen. All three nodded. But it did nothing to help me. I felt no excitement, only trepidation and a sick sense of dread, fear that I would see her and not react. That because of my warped condition, this contamination by Hive technology, the match would be wrong. That this human female would take one look at a broken Atlan beast and turn away, ashamed. And knowing there was one true mate out there for me and she'd rejected me...

"How soon will she arrive?" I asked, swallowing down a sudden lump of fear.

"Any minute now. She is being transported from Earth, so you probably have just enough time to go clean up and put on something less—" Rachel looked me over, head to toe, and she wasn't smiling. "Go put on some real clothes. You look like a walking arsenal. You'll scare the poor woman to death."

The restraints released, and I sighed. I hated being pinned down, just like everyone else on the planet. We'd been shackled by the Hive and integrated to some extent. After escaping, the feeling was not one I wanted to repeat.

I glanced down at my body. At the standard issue Coalition uniform, the weapons that never left my side. Not anymore. Not even when I slept. Losing my beast left me weak, open to attack, and while I was not used to utilizing those tools to assist me in protecting myself, I had no choice. Not with Krael and the Hive lurking in the caves below the planet's surface, slipping through my fingers like water. I could not afford to take chances. I wasn't going back to them. They'd already taken enough. I glared at Rachel. "I cannot protect my mate if I do not have my weapons."

She sighed. "You alpha males are such a pain."

A few weeks ago, her sass would have made me laugh. The other human female I knew, Kristin, often said things of a similar nature to her mates. To which Hunt and Tyran would laugh and drag her to their quarters for private instruction in just how dominant an alpha male could be.

Hunt and Tyran had proved their passionate natures quickly enough. Their mate, Kristin, was heavy with child now, and everyone on The Colony waited expectantly to receive our first new life. Rachel, standing before me with her hand resting on her own, smaller belly, would bring the second newborn baby to our planet not long after Kristin's child was born.

I prayed that Kristin's baby was a girl, that she would be soft and small and beautiful, and remind all of us what we had sacrificed for. Remind us that, even though we had lost everything and been betrayed by our people, there were innocents whom we protected. Beautiful, vulnerable lives who needed us.

Maxim and Ryston stood back, and I was free at last to rise, to walk to the transporter room to meet my mate and hope her presence would be strong enough to overcome whatever evil the Hive had done to me. If not...

I walked out of the medical station and down the hallway, my four companions on my heels as we made our way to the transport room to await this unknown female from Earth. I did not ask for any details from the doctor. Her name. Her age. I did not want to know anything about her. I did not care. She was an experiment. The final test. In the end, she would not be mine. The less I knew, the less I saw, the better for me. Especially, for her.

There were others on The Colony. Other Atlan Warlords who had fought longer or harder than I, who could still summon their beasts. Who could be a worthy mate to a female as fiery or beautiful as the other Brides who had arrived. The fact that my heart did not break told me more than anything just how numb I had become. I had no hope.

3

I STUDIED WARDEN EGARA. SHE SEEMED COMPLETELY CALM AS she talked about the rest of *my life*.

With an alien husband. In space. Although, maybe if he was like the big beast of a man in my dream, that wouldn't be all that bad an option. It beat spending several years in prison, getting out with my career and reputation in ruins. I'd never work on Wall Street again. I'd have to start over. With a criminal record and no friends.

I wasn't a big fan of leaving everything and going into space, but my options sucked.

My breathing was ragged and sweat coated my skin. It felt as if I'd woken from a nightmare, startling and abrupt. But the feelings coursing through me weren't of fear, but of pleasure. It was waning quickly.

I wasn't scared of the dream. I was petrified of what it meant. Why I'd liked it. What he'd done.

No, what I'd allowed him to do. He hadn't raped me. Far from it. He hadn't even really forced me. It had seemed like it, being manhandled, but he'd done it because it was hot. It was what turned him on and he knew his mate would love it, too. And she did—I did—whatever. I'd never had an orgasm like that in my life. Ever.

And it wasn't even real.

"Are you all right?" Warden Egara asked. She sat at the table nearest me, her tablet in front of her. She wore the uniform of the Brides Program, complete with the Interstellar Brides logo that meant she was part of the Coalition Fleet. Her calm, cool gaze helped me breathe. She didn't seem surprised that I'd behaved so unusually during the testing. Had I yelled? Moaned? Screamed?

Had it been unusual?

"Was the testing normal?" I asked, licking my dry lips, wishing I could bury my face in my hands, but the chains running from the padded Velcro straps prevented me from hiding. And suddenly, my nose itched.

Figured.

She cocked a dark brow. "Normal?"

"You know. *Normal.*" I wasn't going to ask her if she knew I'd had an orgasm. If I'd been talking. Begging for it while she sat here with that polite smile and heard every single word.

She offered me a smile, which I had to assume was potentially a breach of protocol. She dealt with volunteers to the program, but also with prisoners like me. I wasn't a murderer or anything, just an idiot who'd gotten greedy and reached for the brass ring. I knew stuff. So did a thousand other people. But they hadn't caught everyone on Wall Street. Just me. White collar crime, doing time for insider trading. Yeah, not my best decision ever, but I was watching the blowhards around me make millions on shady deals, and I'd wanted my piece of the pie.

Seemed I was going to get a big alien cock instead. And after that dream, I was starting to think maybe that wouldn't be such a bad thing.

Maybe that was why I was freaking out about the dream. I didn't let any man have control over me. For any reason whatsoever. I'd been burned by dates. By co-workers. Bosses. Hell, even teachers. But to be sent to prison while the slime I worked with used offshore traders and secret accounts to do the same damn thing...but get away with it?

The whole thing made my blood boil, and I didn't trust men. Period.

"Yes, it's perfectly normal. The testing delves into your subconscious, and we assess your deepest needs and desires to match you to a mate."

I frowned. "I'm not interested in a mate."

She narrowed her eyes as if confused. "You are aware you were tested for the Brides Program, correct?"

I nodded. I couldn't do much more than that, restrained as I was in this weird dentist's chair. I stuck my lip out, blew up my face to move a strand of hair away that was tickling my cheek. "Yes, I know that, but the only requirement is that I volunteer, not that I like the guy."

"Technically, that's true," she replied slowly. Hesitantly.

I sighed. "Look. You know my story. It's all in that tablet of yours, right?"

"Yes."

"So you know what happened to me. Why I'm in jail. Yes, I'm guilty, but there were others far guiltier who got away with it all. Insider trading is bad, but it's not like I killed anyone. I lost everything. My license, my apartment, my friends. I won't be hired anywhere again. Those guys I worked with? They made millions. One of them even bought a house in the Hamptons, and since it's July, I'm sure he's there now. And where am I?" I looked down. "In a damned testing chair. My only options to take control of my life again are to go into the Interstellar Brides Program or rot in jail."

"You could volunteer as a fighter in the Coalition Fleet," she reminded me.

I knew women did that, too. Went out into space and fought the Hive with the rest of the soldiers. I laughed at that. Me, with a space gun? So not happening. I'd be a hazard. "I told you, I'm not a killer. The sight of blood makes me sick. I just want my life back. Or at least my ability to decide what clothes I wear, when I eat. Hell, I would really like a bathroom door."

"You won't be coming back to Earth."

"My choice," I replied. "Don't I have thirty days or something like that? If I don't like him after thirty days, I'm free." That was my real goal. I was a pain in the ass, too brash, too pushy, too much of a bitch to find a man. I was supremely confident this alien wouldn't want me either. Thirty days. I'd get the cobwebs out of my vagina, drive my new alien mate away—as I did every other man—and I'd be home with a nice bit of cash in the bank from the Interstellar Brides Program. Enough to start over. Maybe even start my own financial consulting firm. I couldn't trade on the floor, but there were ways around that. There was always a side door in my business. Always.

And next time, I'd be the one with the fucking bank account in the Cook Islands.

"You'll be matched to a male the computer selects, and you'll have thirty days to accept or reject the match. That is true." Her eyes narrowed, and she tilted her head as if I were annoying her. "This is not a joke, my dear. These warriors are honorable males who have fought and suffered and watched their brothers die. An Interstellar Bride is their ultimate reward. You will be cherished. Adored. Seduced and pampered. It will not be so easy to walk away."

I didn't snort or roll my eyes, but it was difficult. Me? The *ultimate reward.* Poor bastards. "My subconscious might determine where I'm sent, but I'll either like the guy or I won't. This mating will be on my terms."

Warden Egara actually laughed, and I felt my cheeks burn bright red. "You're not very familiar with the males of the Fleet, are you?"

"No. I worked seventy hours a week, focused solely on getting the corner office. I didn't have time to do my own laundry, let alone learn about the men on all of the Coalition planets."

"Yes, that's obvious," she murmured, swiping her finger across her screen. "Males on the matching planets are *very* dominant. They like to be in charge."

I thought of the dream. He'd definitely been in charge.

"Some are from very male dominated societies. Women aren't secondary, they are powerful and adored. But their males are very serious about protecting them."

"I don't need to fight or charge into battle to make up for the fact that I don't have a set of balls, Warden," I countered. That was Wall Street me talking, the woman who'd had to learn to talk like the men, wear a suit of armor and be the bitch to be listened to. "But I do have a backbone. And a mind of my own."

"Trust me, he—or they—will know right off about that."

I knew she was speaking to my more aggressive nature, but I wasn't going to change now. I'd learned not to be a doormat, and I wasn't going back to that scared teenage girl who'd constantly worried about being judged. Been there. Done that. Over it.

My aunt had told me it normally happened to a woman around the age of forty. But since I'd been in banking, in the good-old-boys' club, I'd gotten there early. "And you know this first hand, Warden? How can you sit there and tell me what it's like? Have *you* ever been to one of these planets? Met these males?"

She cleared her throat, tipped up her chin. "Yes, I have. I was matched to a Prillon warrior. I was mated to him and my second for several years before they were both killed in the same Hive battle."

All of my indignant anger fled. "Oh. I'm sorry." I was. I could tell she loved her mates. "I was being bitchy, and I apologize. I admit, I'm nervous. It's scary."

"Yes, it is," she confirmed. "But like you said, you're taking control of your life. Your destiny. You've been matched, and I think you'll be quite pleased. We haven't had a mate reject their match yet."

"No one? Not one woman has said no?"

"No. Not one."

I sighed. "There's always a first time."

She cleared her throat, her brows raised. "You have thirty days to decide, but if you reject him, you won't be coming home."

"What?" This was not what I was expecting to hear.

"You'll be matched to another male from the same planet. The first male is the best match, however, so keep that in mind."

Oh, shit. That fast, this thing had gotten way too real. I'd miscalculated. "What's the match, what planet?" I asked, suddenly nervous.

"You've been matched to The Colony, specifically to an Atlan."

I repeated the planet name, knew nothing about it. A colony? For what?

"Not only do you have a mate, but you'll have to contend with his inner beast as well. I had two warriors. You have one. A very, very big one if he's like all other Atlans. And his beast...I have to assume...will be very dominating and intense."

I remembered the growling. Was the guy from my dream an Atlan?

I swallowed. "Big? As in...everywhere?"

I flushed, and the Warden smiled again. "I would assume so. I have a few questions to finish out the testing. State your name, please."

"CJ Ellison." When the Warden just eyed me, I clarified. "Caroline Jane Ellison."

"Are you legally married at this time?"

"No."

"Children? Biological or legal?"

"No."

"Do you accept the match of the Interstellar Brides Program? Do you agree that you have been matched to an Atlan, have the thirty days to agree to the computer's mate selection or be claimed by him? Do you understand that you will not be returning to Earth?"

"Yes," I replied, for the first time with not much enthusiasm.

Warden Egara nodded, then stood. "Don't worry, you'll be fine."

"You haven't gone back. Is it because you know something I don't?" I asked warily.

She came over to me, swiped her tablet until I heard a whirring in the wall behind me. I angled my head to see the wall had opened and a blue glow was coming from within.

"Yes," she said.

I looked up at her.

"I know how true love feels. What it can be between mates. Hopefully, you will find what I lost."

"But..."

The chair silently slid backward into the wall and

lowered into a warm pool of water. Clearly, Warden Egara was done speaking on that topic.

"Now? I'm not ready!" I wasn't. I needed more time. This wasn't part of the plan. I was leaving. Right now?

Something sharp poked me just behind my ear. I yelped in pain and surprise but it was over in seconds. What. The. Hell?

"Don't worry, that's just the NPU." She didn't even look at me. "Your processing will begin in three...two...one."

4

WE REACHED THE TRANSPORT ROOM AND THE DOORS SLID wide, the Prillon transport officer looking up as if he was expecting us. He was. A set of Atlan mating cuffs was waiting for me as well. He handed the cuffs to me, and I had no choice but to accept them, pinning them to my waist even though I knew I would not have the opportunity to use them.

"Governor." The transport officer nodded at Maxim first, then the doctor, Ryston and me. "Lady Rone." Inclining his head, he bowed to Rachel whose hand rested gently on top of her round, baby bulge. All three of them, the governor, Rachel and Ryston wore matching copper colored collars, identifying them as a mated set. A twinge of envy shot through me at what those warriors shared. A female who loved them. A child. They were a family despite everything that had happened to them during the war. I had no doubt Kristin, Tyran's and Hunt's mate and a member of my security team, would be with us if she were able. But the human woman was on bed rest, the Prillon child she carried about to burst from her body.

Lady Rone smiled at the transport officer, and he stood taller, straighter, his shoulders back.

"We're expecting a transport from Earth," she said.

"Yes, my lady." He looked down at his controls. "A bride from the Interstellar Brides processing center in Miami, Florida, should be arriving any moment."

"Miami?" Rachel asked, her eyes practically glowing. She took a step closer to me again, ignoring Maxim's warning growl. She even shooed him away with her hand. "Oh, behave. Just because I'm wearing your collar doesn't mean you can constantly act like a Neanderthal."

He raised his brows. "What, exactly, is a Neanderthal, mate?"

Rachel laughed. "Knock it off, Maxim." She took my arm, ignoring her mates completely. "Miami. That means she's from the US. Like me."

I knew she expected a response, but I didn't have one to give her. It wasn't like I knew what the US was. Where my bride came from, what she looked like, the very essence of her, was all irrelevant because she wasn't going to be mine. The moment I saw her and my beast remained dormant, I was a dead man. We all knew it, but Rachel was the one who remained upbeat. She had a life growing within her; she was the optimistic sort.

She and the doctor hoped for a miracle. I knew that, but I did not hold such fanciful notions. If the rage that I carried, my hatred for the Hive and what they had done to me had not been enough to trigger the beast, the sight of a beautiful female, a stranger, would do nothing more.

A buzzing energy filled the air as the transport pad came to life. Maxim pulled Rachel backward, her back to his chest, his arms coming around her possessively as Ryston took a step in front of her, blocking her view of the transport pad.

"Get out of the way," she hissed at Ryston's back.

He crossed his arms but did not move. "Not until we know that a bride is the only thing arriving on this transport."

The doctor raised his brow, but Rachel only sighed. "You guys are ridiculous. You do know that, right?"

The governor, Maxim, lowered his head and nuzzled the side of her neck. "It is our job to be ridiculous where your safety is concerned. And that of our baby."

I ignored the byplay, surprised to find that I was actually curious about the woman taking shape on the transport pad. This was really happening. I'd really been matched to a female who was perfect for me. And she was here.

Once the transport began, she materialized quickly, lying on the hard surface. While most transports occurred while one was conscious, the distance from planet to planet, from Earth to The Colony was too great to remain awake.

She arrived wearing an Atlan gown, a dark burnished gold. It shimmered in the bright light. Her hair was long and straight. Sheer black silk so dark it appeared blue when the light reflected off the strands. Her skin was slightly darker in hue than Rachel's or Kristin's, but looked soft. Fragile.

My hand curled into a fist at my side as I fought the impulse to touch her. Her curves were generous, her breasts large. I could tell that she was tall, much taller than the other Earth women who had arrived here. I found that pleased me. For though the Prillon warriors were large, I was half a head taller.

I waited impatiently for her to open her eyes, for her to wake. I knew the Prillon brides usually arrived naked, as was the custom on their home world, Prillon Prime. On Atlan, however, our brides arrived in gowns that hugged their bodies like silk. The material was feminine, soft and inviting, clinging to her curves, so that the Warlord who claimed her, could properly admire them.

Rachel shoved at Ryston's arm, forcing him to the side, not because she was strong enough to move him, but because he allowed it. "Oh, Rezzer, she's beautiful," Rachel said.

The human was right. My mate's face was delicate, with arched black brows and a pouting pink mouth that looked ripe for exploration.

The doctor knelt near her, lifted a wand and did a quick scan. He looked to me, seemingly satisfied as to her health, nodded, then cleared his throat. "Perhaps we should leave Rezzer to his mate."

"Oh, but I want to meet her," Rachel insisted. "She's from home."

Maxim lifted her in his arms, swinging her and her pregnant belly up into his hold as he strode toward the door, Ryston on his heels. "This is your home now, mate. I can see we need to remind you."

"No, really." Rachel laughed and threw her arms around his neck. "I know this is home. But she's from Earth."

Ryston followed them out the door, his eyes heating with a look so filled with desire and expectation that I turned away. I could not stare. I could not stand to look at him. Not when I knew the desire driving him would never be mine.

The doctor looked at me. "Would you like me to stay, perhaps document your reaction?"

I shook my head. I did not need anyone else to witness my humiliation. When my bride awakened, I would tell her that I was broken. Alone. I looked at the doctor. "I will explain to her how things are, and then I will bring her to you, Doctor. She must be matched to a worthy Atlan and—"

He interrupted, shaking his head. "No. She has thirty days to decide. Not you. It is not your decision. That's Coalition protocol. Nothing I can do about it unless you want to take it up with the Prime."

Prime Nial, leader of the entire Coalition of Planets. He'd visited The Colony and was, himself, contaminated. Mated through the Brides Program to a human. He would think me foolish or weak.

Perhaps both. I turned away from the doctor. He chose not to argue further and motioned for the transport officer to follow him out of the room so that I was alone. Staring at her. My perfect match. A woman who should have been mine.

Even though she was right in front of me, close enough I could see her breathing, the little indentation at her elbow, even a perfect little birthmark on her collarbone, the Hive had stolen not just my home, but my future. My mate. *Her.*

Her dark lashes fluttered on her cheeks, and her eyes opened slowly. Blinking like an innocent babe taking in her new world. She recovered quickly, and I admired the keen intelligence I saw coming through her warm brown eyes when her gaze focused on me. I bowed slightly. "Welcome to The Colony, my lady."

She pushed herself up and swung her legs around so she sat with her arms wrapped around her knees and looked up at me. "I'm CJ. Caroline Jane, actually, but my friends call me CJ."

"I am not your friend." I held her gaze not to intimidate, but because I found I could not look away. She was just so lovely and…mine. "I am Warlord Rezzer, Caroline. I am here to escort you to medical."

Her finely arched brows drew closer together. She frowned. The sight oddly enchanting. "What do you mean, escort me to medical? I thought my mate would be waiting for me here. That's what Warden Egara promised me. Have I been transported to the wrong place?"

I held out my hand, worried that she would see right through me, see exactly how broken I was and refuse to even touch me. She studied my open palm just for a second and then placed her warm hand in mine so I could help her to her feet. It was so small, tiny even, in my palm. "There has been an unusual circumstance," I told her as she glanced at me out of the corner of her eye. I assisted her off the platform.

"So you're not my mate?"

I shook my head, ground my teeth together before I replied. "No. We were matched, but I am not able to claim you."

That stopped her cold, and she pulled back on my hand, forcing me to look at her. Into her dark, almost black eyes. If I wasn't careful, I'd sink right in.

"What do you mean? How is that possible? Warden Egara said we were matched."

A bit of the numbness faded but not enough, and I accepted the inevitable—even being near my mate would not be enough to break me free of this new prison. I brought her hand to my lips and kissed it because I needed just one taste before I let her go. "I was captured in the caves beneath the planet's surface a few weeks ago. They—the Hive—did something to me."

She frowned and her eyes filled with worry. All I felt was broken. Ashamed to have to explain my weakness in such detail.

"What? What could be so terrible that you don't want a mate?"

The admission was like acid in my throat, but I forced the words past it. "I can no longer become my beast. I can no longer claim my mate, and so I must allow you to choose another. I must ensure your happiness. You will be mated to a full Atlan. Strong enough to protect you."

Her grip on my hand tightened. "No."

"What?"

"I said no. N.O. As in, no. I do not agree to this." Her soft voice was laced with steel, surprising me.

"I am unfit, Caroline."

"It's CJ," she countered.

My eyes widened at her tone, realizing she wasn't as meek as I'd assumed.

"And Warden Egara said you were my perfect match. The best match in the entire Interstellar Fleet. She said you're mine. If you're mine, you can't just hand me around like a Tupperware dish filled with week-old casserole." She was angry now, her eyes narrowed. The sparks flying from them made her even more beautiful.

I snapped my mouth shut, not remembering when it had fallen open. "What is a Tupperware dish?"

She pulled her hand free and crossed her arms, the swells of her breasts rising with the action. "It's a worthless piece of plastic I use to run science experiments in my fridge. Listen, I'm not a used car. I'm not property. You don't get to just give me to someone else."

I tilted my head, confused by her anger. "Of course, you are not property. You are beautiful. A worthy female. A perfect match for an Atlan Warlord. Which means you are strong, intelligent and courageous. I am unworthy, my lady. I would be selfish beyond reason to keep you."

Some of the anger faded from her dark eyes, and she stepped in front of me, tilting her head back. She lifted her hands to my face, and I allowed her to touch me. To tilt my head down. To pull me to her until our foreheads nearly touched. "What is wrong with you? Exactly?" she asked. "What is so terrible that you would not accept a matched mate?"

"I cannot summon my beast."

"So?"

33

"Without him, I cannot protect you. I cannot fight. I cannot claim you as I would want."

She looked me over, clear skepticism in her eyes. "You look huge to me, like what? Seven feet? Of course you can protect me. Besides, you don't look like you have anything wrong with you."

I shook my head. "You do not understand."

She sighed. "That is obvious. What do I not understand? You're massive. You seem like you can move. What do you mean, you can't fight? You're just going to stand there and let someone like me kick your ass? Or let someone hurt me?"

I knew there was no way to explain it to her. The loss. The weakness. The lack of interest from my cock. So I turned away and opened the door. And I wasn't about to tell her that without the beast, our mating would never be complete. "Come, Caroline. I will allow the doctor to explain it to you."

"CJ." She rested her hands on her hips, her breasts jutting forward beneath the clinging fabric, and my gaze dropped to them before I could think better of it.

For a moment something stirred, something dark and angry and severe. I wanted to reach out and touch the hard peaks of her nipples, taste them, bury my cock in her soft body. I wanted her to heal me. I wanted to be whole. But the flicker inside me soon faded, and I held my hand out into the hall, indicating she should come with me. "This way. Come with me, and I will help you understand."

"No. You seem intelligent enough. You tell me how it's possible the testing system is broken. Convince me that the Brides Program has a flaw. That you aren't meant to be mine." She shook her head, her long, black hair sliding back and forth along her back.

"Caroline," I groaned.

"It's CJ," she said through clenched teeth. "Explain. Convince me. Now."

My mate had a flare of temper, yet so did I. I didn't need my beast to rage for me to be frustrated and mad. Not at her, but the situation we were in. "You want to know? Fine. I'll tell you." I crossed my arms over my chest, mimicking the pose of my matched female. The transport room door slid closed. "The testing proves you not only would be perfect for me, as a male, a warrior, but also that you want to be fucked by my beast. That you would enjoy his dominance, his huge cock filling you up. But I've been damaged by the Hive. No beast means no formal claiming. I can't claim you as is my right as an Atlan. I can't become what I am meant to be because of the Hive. I can't give that beautiful body what it needs."

5

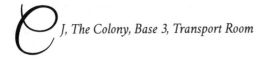

J, The Colony, Base 3, Transport Room

"What do you mean, exactly? You can't have sex at all? You can't get it up?" I asked. This guy didn't look like he had any kind of problems, in any department, especially when it came to sex. And one look at that particular area of his body and—trouble. He was big. Everywhere.

One look at him and my panties would have been ruined —if I were wearing any. He was gorgeous. Huge. Like giant huge. I'd never met anyone so big before. I wasn't small. Not at all and he was a good foot taller than me. I couldn't remember the last time I had to tilt my head up to look at someone. Maybe just before I turned fourteen and hit that one big growth spurt. But that had been over ten years ago.

"Can't get it up?" he asked.

"The big, bad beastly cock. That's what you're talking about? It doesn't work?"

Anger flared in his eyes, but I wasn't scared of him despite the ridiculous number of weapons strapped to his body, or the odd platinum and gray manacles hanging from his waist. The silver hue stirred a memory, but I didn't have time to return to dreamland right now. I had no idea why I wasn't intimidated in the least. If he were to walk down the streets in New York, people would clear the sidewalk for him.

The left side of his neck and lower jaw looked oddly silver, but honestly, it just looked like he'd smeared Halloween makeup on his skin. I didn't know what else might be odd about him, but he was beautiful. Big. And his eyes were a deep, haunted green. So much pain behind them it felt like a gut punch every time he met my gaze. I didn't let him see that I knew, of course. But just arguing with him, I knew I'd never forget him. If I let him walk away now, he'd haunt me. Forever.

So why should I let him give me away? He'd said he was my mate, the one I'd been matched to. Therefore, he wouldn't hurt me. Sure, I could believe the computers, but just looking at him, I knew. It was in his eyes, in the way he looked at me. There was something there, something hurting and lonely and broken. Something I desperately wanted to fix. It was instinct. Pure and simple. He was *mine.* That's what I knew. Deep down. Beyond words or logic or reason. I realized this might be the single most important fight of my life. No way was I walking away.

He was mad, but not at me. He was mad at himself, at his body, which seemed to have recently betrayed him.

"I can get it up, as you call it, but I have no interest in claiming a mate."

"No interest?" I felt my brows go up. He claimed he wasn't interested, but his gaze dropped to my breasts and lingered. I stood straighter, shoving the triple D cups up on display. I ran my hand down my side, to my waist to see if he tracked the movement. He totally did. Not interested? Liar, liar, pants on fire. "You might have low T."

His dark brows went up, and I studied him. From the dark hair that was slightly shaggy—and very silky looking—to his broad shoulders, the form-fitting black uniform did nothing to hide his brawny physique. I glanced lower, to the front of his pants and realized perhaps that wasn't the case. I made sure to hold my gaze there, on the piece of anatomy currently under discussion, and remembered the dream. The huge cock. The grumbling voice of the beast. I made sure he noticed my attention. "Yeah, no. I think you've got plenty of testosterone."

"Female. You are on dangerous ground."

"Apparently not." I pointed at him, circled my finger. "Your beast, in there somewhere, has no interest in me?"

He pursed his lips, glanced over my shoulder, not wanting to meet my eyes. "My beast has been subdued. Perhaps even killed."

My mouth fell open. "I don't understand. Did you have something amputated? Or do you have something dead and rotting inside you? Do you need surgery?"

He stepped closer, his body heat radiating like a warm blanket. He grabbed my hand, placed it flat against his chest. His very hard, very warm chest. I could feel the beat of his heart, the inhalations of his breathing.

"No. He is not dead."

I had a feeling he was saying that more for himself than for me. "Then what?"

"The doctors do not know. They have not identified what has happened to me. This is a first; the first time an Atlan has ever had his beast stolen from him. The Hive did something to me, down in those caves. They *weakened* him so that he can't come to the surface. He is caged. He cannot escape."

"So...you want your beast to come out? Isn't that dangerous?"

"It can be, if I were to go into a rage or mating fever, but for now, I'd do anything to rage. To be able to fight again. I am worthless here. A forgotten relic of the war. I can't fight like this. I can't defend my people. The war rages on, and those of us contaminated by the Hive are banished and forgotten, like broken things tossed in the garbage."

He didn't want a mate, he wanted to go back to war. To fighting and killing. "So you need the beast to come out so you can fight?"

He nodded, a dark curl falling over his strong forehead. "I cannot hunt. I cannot protect a mate or my security team. I am weak."

"How does it normally happen?" I wondered. "When does your beast come out?"

"Several things trigger an Atlan to become his beast. The fever. Anger, especially during battle. Anger at anyone who is harming someone else, specifically my mate. Any threat to the people under my protection, and the beast rises to fight."

"You sound like the Hulk now," I mused, but he ignored my outburst and continued staring at me. "You said something about a fever?"

"Mating fever can summon the beast as well."

"Fever? Taking a mate makes you sick?" That didn't sound promising. No wonder he wanted to give me away.

"When it is time to take a mate, the beast takes control and becomes unmanageable without a mate. A beast in mating fever, with no mate to ease him, means death for an Atlan."

"What? You actually die from this fever?" God, no. That

sounded horrible. What kind of backward place had Warden Egara sent me to?

He paused, taking a deep, shuddering breath. "Without a mate, our beasts are beyond our ability to control. They become destructive. Dangerous. Unmated males in that state are executed."

"What?" He did not just say what I—

"And arousal. Arousal will awaken the beast." He listed all of those items like ticking off checkboxes. Anger. Fever. Arousal. The last bothered me.

"Arousal. You mean attraction to a female can summon your beast? Even if you're not in mating fever?"

He nodded once. "Yes. Although our beasts' response is strongest for a mate."

"That's me," I said. For once in this whole process, I felt unsure. Less than adequate. If I really was perfect for him, as Warden Egara had promised, he should be reacting to me. Wanting me. Turning into his beast so he could shove me up against the wall and... Umm, yeah. *No. Don't finish that thought, CJ. Down that road is trouble.*

I bit my lip and stared up at him. Everything about him made my body feel starved for his touch. I wanted to run my fingers through his hair. Taste his lips. Nibble on his skin. Feel his strong arms around me, his body behind me, over me, in me. Him. I *wanted* him, and I hadn't been hot for a guy in a long, long time. Maybe never. Not like this.

But him? Nothing. He stared at me like he was trying to break bad news to a little girl. An unattractive child whom he had no interest in. And wasn't that just a bitch? "So, I guess I don't arouse you?" Might was well call a spade a spade.

"Ah, Caroline, do not belittle yourself. I am trying to explain this to you. You are beautiful." He lifted his free hand to my cheek, stroked his fingers through my hair. "I am broken."

"You're the one who said a mate should arouse your beast."

"Exactly," he countered.

"But I don't."

"You don't, not because I don't think you're the most desirable female in the universe, but because the Hive broke me. Don't you see? I'm broken. I can't give you what you need."

"So, you're saying you'll never have sex with me?" I was blunt. I'd always been that way, and I had no intention of stopping now. A missing beast? No problem. I could live without a beast. But a lifetime in a marriage to an alien with no sex? I felt robbed. He was so big. And alpha. And smoking hot. Muscles everywhere. His muscles had muscles. I finally find a guy who made me feel small and feminine, and he tells me that he won't touch me? Unacceptable. Seriously. I was going to have words with Warden Egara the next time I saw her.

"I cannot be your mate, Caroline. I am broken."

Broken record. Sheesh. He was huge. Strong. His entire body was lined with weapons. Guns. Knives. He looked like a seven-foot tall Navy SEAL on steroids. If he couldn't fight, then monkeys were going to fly out of my— "So as your mate, it is my job to bring about arousal and anger in your beast."

"It's not your job." He ran his hand through his hair, clearly agitated. I seemed to have that affect on males from *every* planet. "No. It's just supposed to happen naturally."

Great. I'd been on this planet five minutes. All I'd seen was the inside of a windowless room and a hulk of a mate. And we were both just standing here feeling like complete and utter failures. I was supposed to be sexy. Desirable. He was supposed to take one look at me and lose his freaking mind, bend me over a table and grab my hips, pull me back…

No. Not going there.

Too late. My pussy was wet. His hands were huge, and I couldn't stop staring as the matching dream came back to me, playing in my mind over and over like a broken record. I knew what those hands would feel like holding me down. Knew how his cock would stretch me. The way I'd shatter in his arms. I *knew...*

He sniffed, as if he could smell my arousal, his eyes going dark. I was ridiculously good at reading men. I'd dealt with them on a daily—no, hourly basis—and except for the small blip where I was arrested for insider trading, I was pretty good at getting my way.

And right now, I wanted what I'd been promised in that testing chair. Hot, hungry sex with a bossy, dominant male. For real this time. Not just in my head.

This guy, Rezzer, the one I'd been matched to, was truly conflicted. He was pushing me away, not because he wanted to. No, he looked like he wanted me very much. He felt honor-bound to help me find a new mate because he was broken. Very badly. In a way I didn't understand at all but knew it hurt him deeper than any flesh wound.

"Do you have to transform into this beast to fuck me?" I asked. "Can't we just...you know." I held my breath waiting for his answer. I didn't need a beast. But I did need a man willing to touch me.

His breathing changed, just barely, but I heard it. Saw the way the lines around his mouth tightened. The beast that was supposedly dead or dormant or hurt or subdued or something by the Hive? He was still in there. I knew it. Gut instinct told me he was in there. This perceived weakness was temporary.

The real question was, did I want this guy? Did I want him enough to fight for him, for us? Just a little while ago I'd told Warden Egara I didn't have to like my mate. I just wanted off of Earth. Well, that was accomplished. I definitely wasn't on Earth anymore. She'd told me there was no going back. So I'd get a mate. If not this one, another.

But the heart I'd thought too jaded to hope refused to let him go. I couldn't just let him escort me to the doctor so I could get a "better" mate. Not happening. The testing said he was the one. *The. One.* I owed it to myself to see if the program was right. Besides, if anyone was going to push his buttons, make him lose his temper and turn into a raging beast? Hell, annoying arrogant men was my specialty.

He was mine. And now that I'd decided to keep him, it was time for a new approach. So, I'd arouse him. Anger him. I could do that. I'd pissed off enough men on Wall Street to know exactly what to do. The goal with guys was to get them to *think* they had all the ideas when it was your plan all along. Rezzer was the farthest thing possible from a Wall Street executive. I just had to hope that male psychology worked the same here as it did back home.

Remembering Warden Egara's statement about how dominant and possessive the mates were on the Coalition planets, I realized I could use that to my advantage.

I reached up, undid the button at the top of my one-shouldered dress—I'd take the time to figure out how I ended up in such an outfit another time—and let it slide down my body.

"What are you doing?"

"Testing you."

Rezzer's eyes widened and focused on every bit of skin that became exposed. First the top swells of my breasts, then the full orbs themselves with hardened nipples, then my stomach, wide hips, pussy—when had it been shaved?—and then my long legs.

"It's so hot in here." When I spoke, he didn't look up.

Nope, his gaze remained unblinking and centered on my breasts. They were big, like the rest of me.

"I have told you I am unworthy. Why do you taunt me?"

I shrugged, which I knew lifted my breasts. I heard a groan.

I glanced down at his dark pants, saw the outline of his cock against the fabric. I had to assume that was his natural state, that his erection would be even larger, and my inner walls clenched. Already he was big. What would he be like if he were actually aroused…and as a beast?

"What does it matter? You're going to take me to the doctor to pick a different mate. Give me to another. A *worthy* mate. Someone who wants me."

His green gaze lifted to mine for a quick second, then dropped to my navel, then lowered still. I refused to squirm.

"Tell the doctor that my nipples are very sensitive." I lifted my hands up, began to tug the hard tips with my fingers. "I hope my new mate likes playing with them."

They actually were sensitive, and standing before Rezzer was arousing *me*. I wanted him to want me. To have his hands on my breasts instead of my own. I wanted to see more of his cock than just the outline. I wanted to *feel* it deep inside.

"Female, you are pushing me."

"Am I?"

I turned and walked to the door with an exaggerated swing in my hips. "How does this open?"

I wasn't an exhibitionist, not at all. But I was on a new world, and I didn't have to follow Earth rules. I didn't want anyone else to see me, but if this made Rezzer mad enough to touch me, then it would be worth it.

He took two strides and came over to me, put his hand on my arm, and turned me toward him. I looked down at his big hand, so strikingly different than my pale arm. I was toned—

45

exercising every morning at five a.m. before work certainly paid off—but his hands were like dinner plates. *Gentle* dinner plates.

"You are not going out there like that. No fucking way."

Ah, swearing. A good sign.

I blatantly glanced down at his cock, saw that the bulge was bigger.

"I'm not your mate. You said so yourself. You have no reason to stop me," I countered.

He huffed out a laugh. "Oh yes, I do."

I arched a brow, tried my best haughty look. "And why is that?"

"Because until you are assigned to another, you're mine. It is my duty to protect you."

I shook my head, felt my hair slide across my bare shoulders. While the room wasn't cold, it wasn't warm either. His hand, though, was hot, and I wanted to wrap my arms around him and feel his heat.

"You're giving me away."

"Not like this," he growled. "You'll put that dress back on first, and then I'll take you to medical."

"Why? I want as many males to see me as possible, so they know what they might be getting. Those with the most... interest can be on the top of my list."

"List? Do you have any idea what you would cause if you went out there like that?"

I shrugged again, made sure my breasts jiggled with the action. Grinned as they did, indeed, capture his attention.

"There will be an all-out battle. An unclaimed female, naked? I will have to beat them off. You don't want a war, do you?"

I laughed, an honest one. "Me? Start a war?"

"They would take you to the fighting pits. Offer you up as a prize to the victor."

Fighting pits? What kind of crazy ass planet was this? Barbarians Are Us? His nostrils flared and his gaze roamed freely over my body. Lingered. Heated. I lifted my hand to one nipple and rolled it between my fingers. Squeezed as a thrill traveled straight to my clit. I knew my eyes would be wide and dark. I didn't hide what his nearness did to me. Brought up memories of the testing. Lust.

"Fighting? That would be bad, right? Since you can't fight anymore? Although it could be kinda hot, watching them fight over me. No one has ever fought for me before."

It was true. I was tall. Smart-mouthed. Wealthy—until the feds took everything—and mean when I had to be. The men brave enough to date me were few and far between. And not one of them had ever made me feel like this.

His eyes narrowed. Their color went from a deep green to almost black as he watched me play with my breast, transfixed.

"No one will see you like this but me."

"You can't stop me." I lowered my hand and turned toward the door, but I knew I wasn't going anywhere.

"Oh yes, I can."

I stifled a small smile as he played right into my hand.

He spun me back, and the momentum propelled me right into his chest. An oomph escaped me. His hands settled on my lower back, but he turned me even further until I faced away from him. He walked me forward until I was pressed into the wall.

The surface was metallic. And cold. I hissed as my nipples made contact, the memory of the testing dream rushing into my mind. That table had been cold, too. Rubbing my hard nipples. Cooling me in the dream as the heat of the beast at my back had made me come.

Before I could think, he lifted my hands up over my head and secured them with one of his. I was stretched out, his

47

body hard all along my side, my entire length pressed into the wall.

He'd manhandled me to exactly where he wanted me, but hadn't hurt me. I felt dominated, yet protected. My control, which I'd wielded against him like a weapon, was gone.

He was in charge now, and I hoped I hadn't just made a huge mistake.

6

HE HELD ME AGAINST THE WALL, HIS PRISONER. COMPLETELY under his control. The sense of danger, of unease, made my heart race, my breathing hitch. God, I was so wet my arousal already coated my inner thighs. I was hot and aching and empty. Beast or man, I didn't care. I wanted him to fuck me, fill me up. Fingers. Cock. Tongue. I'd take anything he would give me.

Before I could say anything further, his hand came down on my ass with a quick sting. "Hey!" I cried, trying to shift.

"My mate will not behave like this." He swatted me again, harder, sharper. The burn raced straight through me to my clit, and I gasped, nearly sobbing.

"My mate will not expose what belongs to me to anyone else." His hand landed on my bare bottom again. Twice. Three times. Four. Each fiery swat made me twist and writhe in his unrelenting grip, and made me so needy my core throbbed in time to my heartbeat.

"You don't even want me!" I cried out. My butt was on fire. While the swats hadn't been all that hard, his hand was huge. The sting morphed into something more, and I was getting off on this. I liked his domination—just like in the dream.

"Mine." His voice was deeper, rough. Different.

He stilled, his body going tense as his hand settled from swatting my naked backside to petting it. Up and down. Over and over as if he'd never get enough of the feel of my skin.

Mine. The word had slipped out, I was sure of it. I'd riled him up. Pissed him off, pushed him further than I'd pushed any guy before. Hell, no one had ever spanked my bare ass. As if I'd ever let them. But Rezzer had said his beast should want me. The beast the Hive had hurt. That change in his voice, the rough growl, was just like in my dream. Was he changing? Was this crazy idea of mine actually working? There was only one way to find out.

I had to piss him off more.

"Well, you can tell your beast to shove it. I'm ready now. Take me to medical. I'll choose someone else, an Atlan warrior with a nice—"

Swat! Swat!

"Big—"

Swat! Swat!

"Cock."

The last word made him growl, and he moved, plastered his body to my back. He rubbed the front of his pants over my sore, sensitive bottom, the extra irritation only driving me out of my mind. "The only thing my beast is going to shove is a very big cock up that tight pussy of yours. You're wet, aren't you, mate? I can smell your arousal."

His voice changed as he spoke. Deeper. Rougher. And his body *moved*, shifted up and over me even though I knew he wasn't standing on his toes. I looked down and saw his feet firmly planted on the ground. His feet didn't move, so I turned my head and blinked.

He'd grown. Like a foot. His features were bigger. His jaw more pronounced and the section of silver had expanded with him. His brow looked heavier, more primitive. His green eyes were a bit wild, larger, and there was nothing I could recognize as human in them. His teeth were more prominent, pointed. He was huge. Everywhere. Not like before. This was more; like someone had pumped extra mass into his muscles, blown him up until he looked like my personal CGI monster. Like a video game character. One too big to be real. A caricature of himself.

I was looking at a predator. A killer. *A beast.*

My heart raced with panic, faster than a hummingbird's wings, and his touch gentled. His eyes softened. His beast looked his fill, his grip on my wrists steady as iron, but not hurting me.

I was looking at a warrior. A protector. An Atlan Warlord.

Um…wow. This was the beast? Okay. His clothing stretched taut, like putting on little kid's clothes when you're full grown. They no longer fit his frame. I heard rips at the seams, felt the bulge of his cock against my back.

"Mine." The word was barely recognizable, more of a growl. Monosyllabic, as if it were difficult for him to speak in this form.

"Rezzer."

"Fuck you now." He leaned down, *way down*, and smelled my hair like a hunter scenting prey. "Give you big cock." He threw my taunt back in my face, and I would have laughed if his words didn't make my pussy go into spasms, rippling around nothing. Desperate to be filled.

It worked! This had to be his beast. And God, his dirty talk was totally turning me on.

He stepped back, his hand still holding me in place facing the wall as he loosened his pants.

He wasn't kidding. Oh God. He was going to fuck me, right here. Right now. Up against the wall.

I took a slow, deep breath and forced myself to relax as I pressed my forehead to the cool wall. This was what I'd wanted. Rezzer. My mate. Going all beastly and out of control.

But the reality was overloading my senses. He was too big. It was too fast. The rush of pushing his buttons had worn off and now the adrenaline was making me shake. He was a stranger. I was still hot. Still wet. I was aching and needy and empty.

And scared to death.

"Mate." He breathed the word over my skin, his hot whisper on the back of my shoulder sending goose bumps over my body. He stilled behind me, as if sensing the change in me.

He released my hands, and I lowered them to my sides as he took hold of my hips instead. Turning me to face him, he lifted me once more so my back was against the wall, our eyes level.

And yes, he was huge. His face twice the size of mine. His eyes intensely focused on me, reading me, as if he could see into my soul.

I licked my lips nervously as I hung there, unsure what to do until he wrapped my legs around his hips, his heavy erection trapped between us. Unmoving. I couldn't look away from him, from the raw hunger I saw in his gaze. Hunger, and pain. Uncertainty.

Lust.

But his hands were gentle, and he waited; the giant beast of a man waited.

"Rezzer? What are you doing? Why did you stop?" I knew why, but I wanted to hear him say it. No, I wanted *him* to hear it.

"Scared."

One word confirmed everything. His beast was no animal. He was big, but he was mine. He would never hurt me. Not even like this, when I was naked and aroused and half out of my mind. Not even when I was too confused and wild and fearful to resist.

Who was the beast here? The monster? I suddenly had the feeling it was me.

Leaning forward slowly, I pressed my lips to his. I kissed him, and he opened for me so I could explore him in a clash of tongues and teeth and hunger. Just that fast, my body skyrocketed from idle to a high revving engine, and I tore my lips from his with a gasp. "I want you, Rezz. Please. Now."

He didn't talk, but reached to his side and pulled the platinum cuffs free from his waist. I leaned back against the wall, the tip of his cock nestled at my entrance as he separated them and locked the two larger cuffs around his wrists, one then the other.

His gaze lifted to me, and I held my hands out in front of me, eager for this Atlan version of wedding rings. I didn't know anything about them, but I knew they marked me as his. Rezzer as mine. Taken.

A shudder passed through him when the second cuff latched, the seam disappearing. The weight of them was new and, while they were cool, they quickly warmed against my skin. The fit was perfect. He shuddered again. I knew I'd done that to him. Me. The feeling was powerful, an aphrodisiac, and my pussy bathed the tip of his cock with scalding heat.

He growled as I shifted my hips, and I expected him to shove me down onto his cock, hard and fast. Instead, he took my hand and lowered it between us until I gripped his hard shaft. It was so big I couldn't close my fingers around the girth.

I knew what he wanted. He wanted me to guide him inside me, to make sure I was ready, that he wasn't going to hurt me. Somehow, he knew my fear was still close, right beneath the surface. There would be time for rough and hard later. I knew that. And I wanted it. With him. Only with him.

But this first time? I wanted him slow. I needed to look into his eyes and discover him. I needed to look into his soul the way he was looking into mine.

God, he was *huge*. Hot and pulsing in my palm. It had been a while, and I wasn't sure he was going to fit.

But holy hell, did I want to try.

I guided him to me, the large mushroom head sliding past my inner muscles with a pop as he filled me. Stretched me open. Wide. Wider. The stretch was uncomfortable for a moment before I relaxed and used the weight of my body to take him deeper.

He held perfectly still, let me impale myself on him, let gravity do its job. His body was so still he could have been a statue. A tautly muscled, gorgeous statue. His control made me hotter. It made me feel safe, safe enough to let go.

Tilting my hips, I wiggled until he hit my womb, until my pussy was so tight and stretched that I clawed at his uniformed chest, trying to force him to move. I was naked, spread open like a pagan offering, my back to the wall as a beast stared at me fully clothed. Dressed like a warrior. Weapons and blades bumping my thighs as I rode his cock.

What the hell was wrong with me that I thought his guns were hot? That I loved feeling small and helpless and overpowered?

Safe.

There was the word that made me melt into him. I lifted my hands to his shoulders with a soft cry and tried to lift myself up. I didn't get far, but sliding back down was heaven. Pure, fucking heaven.

"Rezzer." I lifted myself again, a little higher this time. Slammed down with a bit more force, made myself whimper as my pussy stretched wider. My juices coating him fully, the glide perfect. Wet. Deep.

Once more. Twice. My breasts rubbed against his uniform, the strange material abrading my sensitive nipples so that I did it more. I needed more.

His gaze never wavered. He watched me with iron control, not even flinching as I lifted myself almost completely off him, my arms shaking with the effort as I clung to him, moaning. Begging him to move. To fuck me. Saying his name over and over as his cuffs seemed to heat against my wrists.

My arms gave out.

His hands were on me in an instant, cupping my ass as he backed me half a step closer to the wall. I was well and truly trapped.

"Yes." I couldn't kiss him now, couldn't stare into his eyes. He was too tall. All I could do was hope he heard me where my face was plastered to his uniformed chest. "Rezzer."

He used his hold on my ass to lift me and bring me back down. Harder than I'd managed. Driving deeper with the slightest bite of pain, of possession, and I moaned. Again. Again.

The chant started in my mind, and I didn't realize I was speaking aloud until he growled the word back at me.

"Mine."

Mine. Mine. Mine. He was mine now.

He increased his pace, pushing my back into the wall to

the brink of pain. The extra sensation simply drove me higher.

"Come, mate. Come."

His rough growl shot through me like electricity, aiming straight for my clit and my body obeyed as he fucked me harder, drove me higher. With the darkest growl rumbling from his chest, he filled me with his seed.

His cock jerked inside me and I lost my mind. I shattered like a broken window. My keening wail a sound I didn't recognize. I was wild, clawing and clinging to him like he was my air, my everything. My inner walls spasmed around him, pulling him deeper, milking the seed from him. My toes went numb, my nipples were painful hard points. The cuffs burned, the extra heat one more flame added to a bonfire.

I was nearly back to myself when he shifted his weight and reached between us to stroke my clit, his cock still buried deep. I was crammed so full, seed slipped around him and down my thighs. His gaze was intent on my face as he continued to master my body. Pushed me to come again.

In seconds, I flew apart.

"Look. Me." He grunted the command when my eyes closed, and I forced them open and held his dark, piercing gaze as tremors raced through me, making me weak. Pliant.

His.

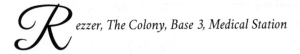

ezzer, The Colony, Base 3, Medical Station

"WHAT THE FUCK DO YOU MEAN IT WORKED?" I HEARD THE booming voice before I saw the governor. "It's been less than an hour."

The leader of The Colony came storming into the private room with Ryston right behind him. Without thinking, I hooked my arm about Caroline and pulled her into my side. While I knew neither Prillon would hurt my mate, my beast acted on instinct.

Yes, my beast. And thank the gods for that miracle.

No, Caroline was the miracle. My personal savior. Just —mine.

As I was sitting on the exam table, Caroline and I were the same height. Her dark gaze held mine briefly before she looked at the duo. She was so lush and curvy, soft where I was hard. But she wasn't small like the other Earth females on The Colony. She wasn't slight. She was quite large—

everywhere. My cock swelled at the feel of her full breasts against my arm. If Caroline stood beside Lady Rone, I would assume she'd be close to a full head taller.

I took a deep breath, caught her scent, the thick musk of fucking lingered on her skin just as I knew my seed coated her thighs. Any Atlan would know she was mine by that alone. My cuffs on her wrists were an outward sign for everyone else.

She was mine now. How stupid and arrogant I'd been to try to walk away from a matched mate. Honorable? No. I'd been an idiot and could have lost her. A growl rumbled in my chest, and she squeezed my hand.

"Governor. Ryston." I angled my head in deference, but didn't get off the table since Doctor Surnen was on my other side waving a wand over me.

"It did work. How fucking big are you?" Ryston asked, a grin spreading on his face.

His gaze raked over me, most likely noticing the ripped clothing...and my size.

"Don't know," I replied. My mate had ruthlessly taunted my beast until it emerged and fucked her. Hard. Once soothed, at least a little bit since her cuffs were on and she was well marked with my seed, it retreated, just enough so I could speak. Could think clearly. Could walk so that my cock didn't lead the way.

I knew the beast was back. I didn't need a doctor to tell me that. Hell, Doctor Surnen took one look at me—and at Caroline—and knew. It was pretty obvious my mate had been fucked, and fucked well. But I wanted to know the beast was back permanently, that she'd fixed me. Or whatever the fuck it was called when she revived my dormant beast.

I wanted to toss Caroline over my shoulder and carry her back to my quarters, keep her beneath me for the next few weeks and make sure she didn't regret allowing me to claim her—but I'd chosen the medical station first. I needed to know what was happening with my Hive contamination, the cyborg parts circulating in my blood. The doctor had never seen anything like it, and somehow the Hive had managed to suppress my beast. Make me weak.

Every Warlord in the Coalition Fleet knew about me by now. The Atlan Senate, the rulers of our home world, were in contact with Doctor Surnen daily, tracking my lack of progress. Even the Intelligence Core, the black ops, assassins and spies of the Coalition Fleet, knew about me.

Not only was I contaminated, banished, but I was such a freak that the entire Coalition whispered my name with fear. Regret. Loathing.

I was the beast who wasn't a beast any longer. Less than a man.

Until Caroline. She'd saved me. Not just my body, but my soul. I could never repay her. But I could damn well try.

Once I had her naked again, nothing was going to separate us. Not even a command from the governor. And the testing chair restraints? They wouldn't keep my beast from Caroline.

And so I sat not-so-patiently, but with keen interest in hearing the doctor's final results.

The governor, Maxim, leaned against the wall next to the door, blocking entrance to anyone he did not authorize. "This needs to be kept off the record, Doctor, until we know what we're dealing with. The extent of his mate's effect on his beast, and until we can figure out how she reversed whatever it was they did to him." His dark brown eyes were pools of death. "The Hive have spies on this base. It's the only way they could be staying one step ahead of Hunter Kiel's security team, the sweeps of the caves. Until we know exactly what's going on, I don't want the truth of Rezzer's recovery to leave this room."

"I agree." Doctor Surnen didn't take his eyes from the scanner in his hand. "And until I know what is going on with his physiology, I don't want too many questions from Atlan or the Fleet either."

Maxim smiled, the look pure predator. "Excellent. We'll both be happier if we don't have to deal with too many questions. At least not yet." He turned his laser focus to me, but the killer was gone, replaced by amusement. "Yes, you said four whole words," Maxim said, a smile spreading across his face. "My mate will be pleased to hear her idea worked."

"Her idea?" Caroline asked. Her voice was raspy, and only I knew it was not her normal tone and the reason why it was that way. She'd screamed so loudly, so deeply when she'd come that it had affected her voice, taken it away. My beast all but preened with that knowledge.

"The testing, Lady Caroline. She was the one who talked Warlord Rezzer into the testing," Ryston added.

Caroline looked up at me, confusion in her dark eyes, and I realized she had no idea who any of these warriors were, nor how much they could alter our fate.

"Mate, this is Maxim, Governor of Base 3 here on The Colony. He is a warrior from Prillon Prime and our elected leader." I cocked my head toward Maxim first, then Ryston, introducing him next. "This is Captain Ryston. He is Maxim's second and they share a mate. Their mate is from Earth, like you." I frowned. "And where is Lady Rone?"

"She is napping." By the smile tugging at Ryston's lips, I had to wonder if it was her mates' attentions that had worn her out or the baby that she carried. Based on the way she'd been escorted from the transport room by her mates, I had to assume the first.

The doctor put down one wand and replaced it with another, holding it up by my head. I ignored the wand and looked at Ryston. "Please tell Rachel that her idea worked."

"The tests are not complete," the doctor said, focusing on his task.

I huffed. "Look at me. It is obvious, is it not?" I was not fully beast, my body having reduced in size as it always did. But I was not fully back to normal, either.

"The testing was all her idea?" Caroline asked.

I looked to her, stroked my fingers down her cheek, gently like an Atlan. "She believed a mate would be able to revive my beast. That a mate would be the only one able to help me heal. While there are a few unmated females on The Colony, none had yet called to my beast to mate. Therefore, they forced me into the testing."

"Forced you?" she asked.

"I can't believe you let me sleep through this," the feminine voice said from the doorway. In strode Lady Rone, her big belly leading the way. "Are you sure, Doctor, there aren't two babies in here?" She pointed to her belly and bumped Ryston out of the way to get to Caroline.

The doctor opened his mouth to respond, but she kept on talking. "I'm so glad you're here. I'd hug you, but that's not really doable for another few months. Another woman from Earth! I'm starting to see a trend."

Maxim put his hand on her shoulder and she quieted.

"Mate, breathe."

She looked put out, but did as told.

"I want to thank you," I told her.

Doctor Surnen put down the wand.

"Well?" I asked him.

"I see no lingering effects of the Hive protein synthesis in any of the tests. They were there earlier and now? Not a trace. I don't yet understand how this happened, but your mate has successfully revived your beast."

"I'm cured?" I asked.

Everyone was focused on the doctor. "While I have no

idea what the Hive actually did to you during your short captivity, the scans indicate your physiology has returned to normal. I cannot say for certain that the condition will not return. I'll need to run more tests. But, as of this moment, the only traces of Hive in your system are the auditory implants and flesh integration that began during your original captivity."

And *that* was the reason I was here. On The Colony in the first place.

Contaminated.

I lifted a hand to my neck, the side of my jaw where I knew my skin there was no longer fully Atlan, but Hive. I had no idea what they'd done to me, or what the end game had been, but that part of me was permanently changed. Silver. Odd. And I could hear better than any other Atlan out of my left ear. I could hear every heartbeat in the room. I'd learned to ignore the overload of sound, unless I was with my mate.

And the sounds I heard were her pulse, her cries of pleasure. She turned and lifted her hand to cover mine, to the mark of the Hive on my flesh. There was no disgust or judgment in her eyes, just acceptance. Tenderness. Compassion.

I wanted to see love there. I wanted her to look at me the way Rachel looked at Maxim and Ryston. But I hadn't earned that yet. But I would. I would make her whimper and moan and lose control. I would make her mindless with pleasure until she thought of nothing but me.

Gods, yes, I would listen to her for hours.

"Listen, Rezzer. This is good news, but as I have no idea how they managed to suppress your beast, I have no way to be certain the effects will not return, that there isn't some hidden, microscopic implant capable of regenerating. They did something to you on a cellular level. I need more time."

"When can I return to working with Hunter Kiel, Captain Marz and the security forces? I need to find the Hive and eliminate them. I need to return to the caves, the hunt." Gods, the thought of it made my heart beat faster. I was born to fight. I was a Coalition fighter and would always be one. Nothing could stop me. And now that I had a mate to protect, I would be relentless. Could spend hours in the caves. The traitor, Krael, and his Hive minions would die. "I'll tear the Hive in two with my bare hands. I'll—

Caroline pulled away from me. "No."

I stilled as that single word sliced through me like the largest Atlan blade. "What?" My beast began to prowl, and I felt my spine tingle, ready to lengthen further. "No? I will protect The Colony, mate. I will protect—" I'd been about to say I would protect *her*, but the doctor cut me off this time.

"No, Rezzer. Your body might not keep you from returning to your role with The Colony forces as an Atlan Warlord, but your cuffs will."

I glanced down at my cuffs, at those about Caroline's slender wrists. "Fuck." Gods be damned. I was blessed, and cursed. I was leashed like a dog now, but couldn't make myself regret it. The beast, however, growled from deep within.

At the sound, Caroline stepped back, lifted her hands. "What's so special about the bracelets?"

I chuffed out a quick laugh. "They aren't bracelets. They're mating cuffs."

As she frowned, Ryston said, "Just take them off, Rezz. You can control your beast. You didn't have Mating Fever. Hell, you didn't even want a mate. We had to hold you down in the testing chair. You fought us every step of the way."

Caroline's lip trembled and she was wringing her hands in front of her waist, the small tell making me want to pull her close and comfort her. Before I could stop the fool, Ryston kept talking.

"You said you were going to give her up. Now you can. You can go back to hunting with the security team and Caroline can choose another."

My beast did come out then. Within two seconds, I grew. Big. So big that Ryston's eyes widened, and Maxim yanked their mate behind him.

"Oh, he's healed, all right," Rachel said with a laugh. However, she was the only one in the room who was the least bit amused.

"God, all I hear is how much you didn't want a mate!" Caroline's voice cut through everything else. The beeping of the machines in the other room, Maxim arguing with Rachel to stay behind him, the doctor telling me to calm down.

Her tone was quiet, but there was steel behind the words. Her shoulders slumped in defeat as she reached for the cuffs on her wrists. "Fine. Here. Take them off. Go hunt, or fight, or whatever it is you want more than you want me."

I whipped my head toward Ryston, wished looks could kill.

"No. Mine." My beast wrapped his hands around her cuffs, holding them in place. I needed more than single words to tell her what she meant to me now. What a fool I'd been, believing, even for a moment, that I could resist her. Not want her. I'd been irrational.

I took a deep breath, then another, willed my beast back, but I could still speak with simple words. Now that she'd lured the beast out, revived him, whatever it was that my mate had done, my beast was back in full. Rested. Eager. Ready to claim.

"You said you were giving me to another because your beast was gone. You were being honorable." She twisted her wrists to get away from me, and I didn't want to scare her, didn't want to be the kind of mate who forced his will on a female. Not now. Not ever. No matter how much she hurt me.

She backed further and further away from me. "But you didn't want a mate at all. They had to—hold you down? Literally, strap you to the chair and force you to go through with it?"

Fuck. Her eyes were round, glassy as if she were going into shock. Tears fell from them as she blinked, sliding down her cheeks. Gods save me. She lifted trembling fingers to each side of her face and wiped them away as if they were acid on her skin. I relaxed my muscles, opened my fingers from the tight fists, tried to speak and explain with more than the one syllable words I was capable of when my beast was in charge. But with each step, he grew stronger, not weaker. My mate was hurting. In trouble. Lost. And my beast raged with helplessness. Every instinct I had was to scoop her up into my arms and take her away to a hidden place, somewhere where I could curl my body around her and keep her safe. Warm. Mine.

"First, Ryston's an asshole," Maxim stated, interceding on my behalf, and I had to agree. Ryston was hurting my mate with his claims.

Except his words were truth. I had not wanted a mate. They had forced me to be tested, strapping me down and holding me there against my will.

"I'll agree to that," Rachel chimed from behind Maxim's back.

"Mate," Ryston said slowly in response, that one word a clear warning, to which she crossed her arms above her big belly and scowled right back at him. She knew she was safe, that her mate would never, under any circumstances, harm her. Just as I would never hurt Caroline. Except, now I had.

Lady Rone had been claimed by her mates in the

traditional Prillon ceremony. Their collar was around her neck. She wasn't going anywhere. They could argue all they wanted, their relationship was solid. Permanent.

But Caroline had only been with me for a matter of hours. Yes, we'd fucked. She wore my cuffs. But she had thirty days to walk away from me. To leave me. To judge me unworthy. She wasn't truly mine. Not forever. Not yet.

I closed my eyes and breathed, willed my beast back. When I felt my beast retreat, allowing me to take control, I looked at Caroline again. She was waiting, another tear sliding down her cheek.

"I didn't want a mate," I said. "That's the truth. But only because I was broken. I had no beast. I was no good for you."

Caroline crossed her arms over her chest. "Now, though, you're all better. Your beast is obviously back. You can go to battle or whatever it is you do. If you didn't want me, and didn't want to give up fighting, go ahead. I won't stand in your way."

She was blunt and abrasive and my beast loved that. I had to assume that was part of the reason he'd come back. But this tone? It was defensive. She was pushing me away to protect herself. I didn't like it. Not one bit. It was my job to protect her.

"Did you want me, Caroline? Did you run to the testing center to be matched? Were you a volunteer for the Brides Program?"

She glanced at the ground, then at me. "No."

"You had no choice, same as me." I angled my head toward the others. "They forced me into the testing chair."

She laughed. "How? With tranquilizer darts?"

"I'm big, but without my beast, they were stronger." I narrowed my gaze at Ryston. "No longer." Fair warning, fucker.

"I chose to be a bride instead of going to prison. I was

tested, yes, but I had the final say. No bride from Earth can be matched without her consent."

"That's true," Rachel murmured.

My beast groaned. I couldn't tell the governor or his mate to leave, or to fuck off. I had to tolerate their presence.

"It's obvious that you're done with me," she continued. "You got what you wanted. You got a quickie, and you got your beast back. Congratulations." She didn't sound pleased at all. She sounded pissed.

"There is nothing quick about what I have planned for you. I will not leave you, mate." My voice was clipped. Dominant.

"Then I will leave you." She strode to the door, looked left and right for something, but when it slid open silently, she all but ran through. Then she was gone.

"Aren't you going after her?" Maxim asked, staring at the door as it closed once again. "She has no idea where she's going."

I slowly shook my head. "She won't go anywhere." I held up one hand, reminded them of the cuffs. My beast did not like our mate's anger, but he, too, was content to wait, to let her learn this one lesson on her own. No warrior on the base would harm her, not with my cuffs around her wrists. And the cuffs had one more failsafe, one more way to make sure a beast could survive the Mating Fever. "I give her three seconds."

Everyone waited silently. The electrical surge hit me like an ion cannon, stronger than what she would feel, strong enough to remind a raging beast to fight for sanity, to go after his mate. To wrestle the demon back from the edge. The cuffs were a safety feature designed to keep rampaging monsters, Atlans in the throes of Mating Fever, from losing themselves, losing control. But the jolt was not one-sided. We could not afford to have our mates far from us when the beast prowled so close to the surface, when a mate's soft voice, her touch, were the only things the wildness inside would respond to. When she was the only thing that stood between a beast and his execution.

I winced, not at my pain, but for hers. The others cringed when we all heard her muted yell.

I stood. "Thank you, Doctor, for confirming what I already knew. Governor, if you'll excuse me, I have a mate who needs answers."

My leader nodded and I left them, quickly finding my mate on the floor in the hallway just outside the medical station. I knelt beside her. "Better, mate?"

The pain was gone now that we were close once again.

"What the fuck was that?" she asked, turning her face up to mine. She held one of her wrists in her hand, her palm gripping the cuff.

"These are mating cuffs. We can't be far apart without it causing us both pain."

"You felt it, too?"

"Of course." That seemed to mollify her somewhat.

She continued to glare at me, a fresh wave of tears gathering in her eyes. "Good."

"My apologies, my lady. I have not handled this, you—" I sighed. "—us very well."

"No shit, Sherlock."

I frowned at the Earth term, but picked up her meaning.

"If you don't want a mate, why am I wearing them?" she asked.

Huddled on the floor, her long dress billowing around her, she looked so beautiful, but so lost. It was difficult to remember that the strong female who'd coaxed and prodded and tugged my beast out was also new to the planet. New to everything around her. Including me.

"My beast put them on you. He is very possessive. And I have discovered that I am as well."

"Yeah, right." She turned her head away from me and wiped at her cheek. She was hurting. Unacceptable.

"I will explain everything in my quarters. Will you permit me to escort you there?" When she remained silent, I added, "Please."

That seemed to have worked, for she put her hand in mine. The connection, just through our fingertips, was enough of a reminder of why I'd been so fucking wrong. I wanted her. With a vengeance, and I would claim her. Keep her. Never let her go.

I *would* have her heart for my own. Heart. Body. Soul. She was mine. All of her.

8

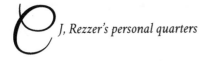

J, Rezzer's personal quarters

I WAS TURNING INTO A BITCH, A WHINY, EMOTIONAL WRECK. I was overly sensitive and angry, a nag. I felt used. I had a little bit of an excuse. I'd traveled to a new world. Met a mate who didn't want me, who'd tried to give me away. I'd taken a chance, risked everything to coax his beast from him. I'd given a complete stranger control of my body. Let him use me. Fuck me. Fill me with his cock. And then? Celebrate the fact that I had a magic pussy; that I'd healed him somehow and now he could *leave me and* return to battle?

What. The. Hell?

I didn't understand any of this. So, yeah, it had been a big day.

But the one thing I didn't like was to be used. Used and tossed aside. The greedy executives at the top in my company had done that to me. I'd been used in the insider-trading scheme and paid the price. They'd walked away scot free, abandoning me to the courts, to a cruel fate in prison. Yes, I was guilty. But we were *all* guilty.

And now, now that I'd fucked the beast back to life, he was going to toss me aside and go back to his old life. Like I was nothing more than a tool. Medicine? His last chance?

Not happening.

I took in his quarters. They were like a modest hotel suite without any charm. Simple. Plain. Basic. The bed, though, was huge. Bigger than any I'd ever seen, but it made sense since he was bigger than anyone I'd ever met.

When Rezzer said nothing, I turned around. He leaned against the wall just inside the closed door. His beast was gone, and he was now his normal size, which was still huge, and muscled, and totally freaking distracting. The clothing that had stretched taut around his beast now barely clung to his frame once more. He looked rumpled and sexy, well fucked. Pleased with himself. Which was completely unfair when I was questioning everything, feeling like an idiot, a hopeless romantic, emphasis on hopeless.

Scratches marred his right cheek, red against the dark stubble. His green eyes watched me closely, his arms folded over his broad chest. He was gorgeous.

I sighed because, while I was upset and hurt, I still wanted him. My pussy ached from the size of his cock and his seed still slipped from me. He was quite virile and I felt the pull of his animal magnetism. Moth, meet flame. He was going to burn me to ash.

I didn't even mind the feel of the bruises along my back from being pounded into the hard transport room wall, or the ones I knew would be on my bottom from his hands.

"You were a fighter? In the war?" I asked, running my fingers along the top of the small table.

"I am an Atlan Warlord. I fought for seven years before

the Hive captured me. Killed thousands of them." He sounded oddly proud of that fact, and my heart sank.

"You loved fighting, didn't you?" I asked, but I already knew the answer.

"Yes. We are born to fight, Caroline. But I was tired. We're all tired. This war has been going on for centuries. Since long before I was born."

"So, why are you here? Why am I here? You can't fight anymore because your beast was gone?" We stood facing each other across the room, the tension, the attraction so thick in the air it was like breathing taffy.

"I fought. I was captured and tortured. But I was one of the lucky ones. I survived. All they left me with was this." He pointed to the silver flesh on his left side. "Others suffered worse fates, were absorbed into the Hive mind. Lost forever. But those of us here, on The Colony, managed to escape with our minds intact."

"Everyone on The Colony has Hive implants?" The idea was disturbing, but I couldn't quite put my finger on why. My mind was trying to assimilate what he was telling me. What small amount Warden Egara had told me.

"Yes. We are all contaminated."

"Contaminated?" What the hell kind of word was that? "I don't understand. Contaminated with what? Poison? Are you all sick? Do you have some strange disease? What are you talking about?"

He sighed, the look of defeat in his eyes one I recognized from earlier, in the transport room, when he'd been trying to tell me he was unworthy. I didn't like it.

"We are all here because we have Hive technology integrated into our bodies that cannot be removed. We are considered a danger to our people, our planets. And so we are banished to live out the rest of our lives here, on The

Colony, with the others who carry the curse of their time with the Hive in their flesh."

"Why here? I don't understand why you all can't go home." This was—a disgrace. That's what this was. War heroes. Soldiers who fought and died and suffered. And now they were *banished* forever from their homes because of a silver eye, like Ryston, or silver skin, like Rezzer? "That's total bullshit."

He sighed. "Here, on The Colony, we are deep inside Coalition space. The communication frequencies that the Hive use to control their Soldiers and Scouts can't reach us here. But if we went home, or back to our battlegroups?" He shrugged. "Every warrior here has the potential to be used by the Hive, taken over, reactivated, forced to kill our own people. Our friends. Our fellow warriors. We are not children with scars, mate. We are hardened warriors, battle tested. Killers. We all understand why we are here. We have accepted the sacrifice we make to protect our homes, our people."

"That's not right," I protested. I couldn't wrap my mind around this. Banished, like lepers? These were warriors who'd paid the ultimate price, risked everything, and they couldn't even go home?

Was that why so few human soldiers had returned to Earth? We'd been under Coalition protection for just over two years now. The length of time the soldiers were required to volunteer to fight. And yet, I'd only seen one or two return. Every time one of them made it back, the news channels blasted it all over the planet like it was a major news story. "Are there human soldiers here? People from my planet? From Earth?"

He nodded, slowly. "A few. Not many. Humans are fierce fighters, small and fast. They are placed on ReCon teams, infiltration and stealth units. But when they are captured, most don't survive."

My hand moved to cover my stomach. I was going to be sick. "This isn't right. It can't be right—"

"It's war, Caroline. It's dirty and ugly and terrible. The few who survive are kept alive by hope."

My head snapped up at that, but his gaze was solemn. Serious. "I don't understand."

"Coalition fighters who complete their service are eligible for the Interstellar Brides Program matching protocols. We are promised a perfect match, a mate who will accept us, love us, allow us to pamper and protect her, love her, give her our seed. We are promised a future that isn't dirty or ugly, but soft and beautiful and perfect. That is why you are here. That is where most other Warlords find the will to fight, to survive. For the promise of a mate like you."

"Other warriors? What about you?"

"I am not like the others. I never imagined claiming a female as my own. I am not worthy of you. I fought because it is my nature to protect my people, because I cannot surrender to the enemy. I am stubborn and merciless, Caroline. I am as ugly and terrible as the Hive who tortured me. I am a beast. I kill without remorse or regret."

"And now? What about now? Do you still think you are unworthy?"

"Yes." He reached for me. Stopped. "But I am not strong enough to give you up."

My heart was breaking. Melting. Reforming into something I didn't recognize. For him. God help me, I was falling in love with him. Right here, in this stark room on an alien world, talking about death and torture and banishment.

And hope. His words were raw and honest, and I swayed on my feet, dizzy and overwhelmed with what he said to me, the power he handed me to break him. It was too much. "The doctor said the Hive protein or whatever was gone. Out of your system. So why can't you go home?"

"Because I still have this." He pointed to his neck. "The integration with my biological tissue is complete and deep. The Hive enhanced tissue runs through half of my neck, to my major arteries, even to the nerves on the edge of my spine. Removing it all would kill me."

My mouth fell open. "Wait. The Hive did *that* to you? Made your skin silver?"

He frowned. "Of course. Almost all Hive integrations are this color."

"I just thought…well, I just thought you were born that way. Aliens on Earth are often depicted with…stuff like that. And the others? Ryston's eye? The doctor's hand? The governor? His skin is copper colored, and beautiful, except—"

"His arm. And his skin is not beautiful, mate." Rezzer's small jealousy was kind of adorable, so I was grinning when he took me to the dark side. "I was captured by the Hive twice. The first time, they did this." He touched his jaw. "It does nothing. I don't feel it. The implant in my ear gives me excellent hearing, almost as good as an Elite Hunter, so I do not complain. I was lucky. I escaped before they could do worse. But I am on The Colony because of it."

"They captured you twice? And you escaped *twice*?" Holy shit.

"Yes. It is my greatest failure as a warrior."

I frowned. "Um, no. It shows how strong you are. Brave. To escape the Hive twice. Wow." I was amazed. And a little proud of him. Scared, too. I could only imagine what he'd gone through. Hive silver? All the way from his jaw to his spine? I shuddered.

I cleared my throat, changed the subject. "So now what?

All the warriors, the fighters, just come here to work and die?" I asked.

He shrugged as if he didn't care. "For decades that was our fate. But then the Prime on Prillon, their ruler, lost his son, Nial, to the Hive. When Prince Nial returned, he was one of us."

"Is he here?"

"No. His father was killed and the planet, the entire Interstellar Coalition, would have been lost without a strong successor. He took his second, a warrior named Ander, and traveled to Earth to claim his matched mate before challenging the leaders of Prillon Prime in the public arena to reclaim his throne."

"She's from Earth, too?" The ruler of the entire Coalition Fleet was matched to a human? That was one woman I really, really wanted to meet.

"Yes. And a warrior. She said she was in your American Army."

"Have you actually met her?"

"I have not. But her name is Jessica. She came to The Colony with Prime Nial and Ander to celebrate the arrival of Lady Rone, the first matched mate to come here once the ban on brides for The Colony was lifted."

My heart raced. Jessica? Was he serious? "She's from the US?"

"What is U-S?"

I waved my hand to dismiss the question I'd asked. "And? What happened? Where is she now? Where is your prince?"

"He is now Prime Nial. He rules Prillon Prime and is commander in charge of the entire Interstellar Coalition Fleet. His cousin, Commander Deston, leads the war effort while Prime Nial deals with all of the Coalition worlds' rulers and laws. He rules the Interstellar Coalition of Planets. We all answer to him and his laws. His mate, Lady Deston, gave us a new designation. We are no longer referred to as the contaminated. We are now veterans. Prime Nial also lifted the banishment, allowing us to return to our home worlds."

Now I was really, really confused. "Then why are you here? Why is anyone still here?" I would have been out of here so fast, their heads would still be spinning. Home. Green grass and trees and blue skies. Chocolate and apple pie and Mexican food. Movie theater popcorn and sitcoms.

"The work we do here is needed. We could go home, but just because the Prime allows us to leave, does not mean we would be welcome on our home worlds. People fear us and our cyborg implants. We are different. We frighten the women and children and make the other warriors uneasy. Rarely will a female choose a contaminated warrior for a mate. It simply is not done."

"But—"

"No, Caroline. Hope is worse than acceptance. We are useful here. We serve. We sacrifice, and we live the best we can. We protect resources vital to the Fleet. We still have a job to do here. If we went home, we would be…nothing. Invisible."

"You're too damn big to be invisible."

That made him chuckle. "I am average size for a Warlord."

"You said Warlords get mates. So, they call you Warlord Rezzer," I said, testing it out on my tongue.

He tipped his head slightly. "And you are Lady Caroline."

"Lady?"

"All mated females are referred to as Lady. It as a term of the highest respect."

"But I'm not mated."

His green eyes narrowed, focused on me as if he had laser beams coming out of his eyeballs. "You are. The cuffs on your wrists mark you as mine. The seed slipping from your core mark you as mine. You are mine."

I looked away. "But you don't want me."

He pushed off the wall, came over to me. Loomed. "That is where you are wrong. I didn't want to be tested. But I've been yours since the moment I saw you. I do not deserve you, but I will not give you up."

He said nothing more, and I turned away, unable to believe him, no matter how much I wanted to. "Is that a window?" I asked, pointing at the space on the wall beside the table. It looked like some kind of curtain blocked out the outside, and I needed a distraction.

Rezzer reached out, touched a small button on the wall and the blind slowly rose, revealing the planet outside, The Colony to me for the first time.

I walked over and put my hand on the glass, stared outside. The landscape was barren and rocky, the ground a scorched mix of reds and brown stone with ragged looking vegetation fighting for life in twisted displays of tenacity. It reminded me of pictures I'd seen of the red deserts of Arizona. The sage. The cacti. I wondered if they had scorpions here. Or snakes.

"Is it anything like Earth?" he asked from behind me.

I realized he'd remained quiet as I saw my new world for the first time. I shook my head. "Not where I lived. My view was buildings. Buildings that touched the sky. Eighty floors and more. Concrete everywhere. No green. Swarms of people. I lived in a city. But I've seen pictures of places like this."

"I don't think I'd like that much. Atlan, where I grew up, is green. Verdant. Open." His hand came down on my shoulder, squeezed gently. "Caroline, I didn't want a mate. That is true. But I want you."

I let my fingers slide down the glass. "What's the difference?"

"A mate was any female in the universe. *You* are one of a kind. Mine."

I thought about that as he continued.

"I can see now that you intentionally prodded me, made me angry, coaxed my beast. It worked, and for that I will be forever grateful. Why did you do it?"

I turned then, tilted my chin up to look at him. He pulled a chair out from the table and sat down. "Better?" he asked.

I nodded, thankful I didn't have to crane my neck.

"Why, Caroline?"

I sighed, starting to like that he didn't call me CJ. "Because when you said you'd take me to the doctor where I could choose another, you were being noble, thinking of me, not yourself."

"You stripped naked because I was noble?" he added.

I blushed at that, remembering my boldness. I wasn't feeling so bold at the moment. "I wanted to help you. And I…"

"You what?"

He'd bared his soul to me. How could I do less? "I didn't want to give up the hope either."

"What hope? What was your dream? Your heart's desire?"

I sighed, suddenly feeling gullible again. Like a fool. "Warden Egara, well, the whole Interstellar Bride Processing Center actually, has been doing a really good job of recruiting mates. Promising the women something that seems impossible for someone like me."

He frowned. "I don't understand."

And—here we go. "I'm too tall. I'm too big. I have a big nose and a round ass and most men are either intimidated by my bank roll, my education or my attitude. No one wanted to date me. I was alone all the time. I wanted…a different life."

"A mate."

I had no idea why that one word made my cheeks heat, but it did. "Yes. A mate. And Warden Egara promised me that the matching protocol worked. That out of every single man in the universe, you were the perfect match for me. And I just wasn't willing to give that up without a fight."

"That's why your pussy was wet when I held you against the wall?" His voice tipped low.

I had to look away, no longer able to meet his eyes. "I was aroused because I wanted you. Because your strength is intoxicating. I love your muscles and your guns and the way you—"

Lifting his hand, he placed one finger under my chin and lifted my face to his. He was doing it, right now. And I couldn't finish the sentence.

"The way I what?"

"Look at me like you want to—"

He completed the sentence for me and my pussy was wet and hot, aching by the time he was done. "Fuck you. Taste you. Devour you. Possess you. Protect you. Feed you. Make you whimper and beg. Make you scream my name as I fill you with my cock. Give you my seed. Mark you. Claim you. Make you mine forever?"

"Yes. All of those things."

"And I want to do them all." He stroked my hair back from my face, gently tucked it behind my ear. "And what do you want?"

I blinked. Dangerous. Dangerous. Dangerous. Why was I telling him all this? "You." Simple answer. Complicated, too.

"There you go, mate. You wanted *me*." I saw relief in his dark gaze, and a bit of pain, too. He was a huge warrior, but

I'd managed to hurt him. "Would you really have walked naked through the corridors in search of another?"

Remembering my taunting words, I shook my head. "No. I wanted you."

"And I want you."

Hooking a hand around my waist, he tugged me toward him, and I fell onto his lap. The feel of him, so big and warm and gentle, was comforting. For once, I felt quite small.

I sighed again, put my head against his chest. Just breathed, took in his scent, the feel of his heartbeat against my cheek.

I couldn't miss the thick prod of his cock against my thigh or the way my mind wandered, filling my head with nothing but images of him as he'd looked thrusting into me, his beast's eyes wild and gentle all at the same time. God, it was addicting being looked at like that.

"This is crazy," I said, after a time.

"What?"

"Wanting you this much. I don't even know you."

"Then we shall fix that." His hand slid up my back to the base of my skull where his huge fingers rubbed the sore muscles there with a tenderness I'd never felt before. "I will take care of you now, mate. Let me."

I relaxed into his hold, completely under his spell. "What do you mean?"

"A bath. Food. Talking. I would learn you as well. I must know everything about you."

My eyes fluttered open to find his green gaze fixed on me with something close to complete and total worship in his eyes. He was serious.

"I'm not that interesting," I muttered.

"You are fascinating, Caroline. I would know what you love. What you hate. Your favorite dishes. What you like to do. What makes you laugh." He leaned closer, his lips grazing my cheek. "Where you like to be touched. What makes you whimper and beg and scream."

He pulled back and our gazes locked. I forgot to breathe. I had never seen that look in a man's eyes before, and it made my insides shift, my chest grow tight. What the hell was he doing to me? "Are you a hypnotist or something?"

His frown was genuine, and adorable. "I am a Warlord. I do not use mind control trickery on a female."

He stood then, carried me as if I were as light as a feather to a bathroom that I was excited to see appeared completely modern. He settled me on the edge of a bathtub and turned on steaming hot water. He frowned, looked at my skin, and reached in to make the water cooler. "You are too delicate for such heat."

I laughed at that. "I'm no hot-house orchid."

His fingers trailed over my shoulder to the clasp on my dress. As I'd done earlier, he released it and pulled me to my feet. The dress slipped from my shoulder to pool on the floor. "Do you need my assistance with your bath?"

Oh, boy. But no. I was sore. Tired. Hungry. And feeling *way* too vulnerable to let him get inside me again so soon. I needed to gather my wits and rebuild some defenses around my stupid heart. The cuffs might force him to stay with me, and me with him, but I couldn't get over Ryston's reminder that they'd had to hold Rezzer down, force him to submit to the testing. That even after my arrival, he'd been in a big fat hurry to give me away. That now that he had his beast back, all he wanted to do was go back to war. To fighting and killing. To hunting down Hive on some kind of security team.

I shook my head. "No."

His silence stretched as the tub filled, and I knew he was watching me, trying to read me. But I hadn't spent all that time on Wall Street without learning how to put on a poker face. My adolescent demonstration of nerves and drama was over. I was a full-grown woman, not a fourteen-year-old who couldn't get her emotions on lockdown. I didn't do drama. Hadn't for years.

Not until him. And these people. And the human woman, Rachel, and the beautiful round belly that had hit me like a punch to the gut.

Babies. God, I hadn't dared let my mind go there, not for years. But the idea of holding a child, a little one with my black hair and Rezzer's green eyes? The need made me ache, an actual hole opening up inside me that I had never felt before. An emptiness I now knew needed to be filled. Wanting children was a weakness I'd refused to allow myself to think about on Earth. No husband, no prospects. That meant no children, because I sure as hell didn't want to raise kids alone. Too hard. Way too fucking hard. I knew single mothers who did it, and they scared the shit out of me. They were stronger than I. They had to be. Raising children was one battle I'd never been willing to fight alone.

Now? With Rezzer? I ran my hand down to my abdomen, realized that he'd fucked me without protection. I'd never had sex without protection before. Never. But to say the beast had made me forget…well, that was an understatement. I'd gripped that big cock and all rational thought had fled. Since I was no longer on birth control—it wasn't something they handed out in prison—I could, at this very moment, be on my way to carrying his child. The thought both thrilled and terrified me, and I hated that weakness in myself.

He turned off the water, the tub full of steaming bubbles that smelled wonderful, like rose petals and lemon drops, and stood. "I will have a meal ready for you, mate."

I nodded, but waited for him to leave the room before sliding into the warm water.

The heat soaked into my muscles and I leaned back,

resting my head on the edge of the tub. Paradise. This moment was paradise.

My beast left the door open, and I wasn't sure if it was for me—so I'd know he was near—or for him, so he could keep an eye on me. Either way was fine. I didn't care. He'd seen me naked. Fucked me. I was past being modest. I rather enjoyed hearing him moving around in the next room. Strange aromas filled the air and my stomach responded with a series of hungry growls that had me standing, dripping water and looking around for a towel.

Stupid. There was nothing. Why hadn't I asked for one *before* I got into the tub?

As if he'd been waiting, Rezzer was there. He'd changed clothes, wearing loose-fitting brown pants and a shirt that looked like they were softer than my skin. I wondered if those were his pajamas, or if he slept naked. He lifted me from the tub and wrapped me in a giant, fluffy blanket that whisked the water away from me. I thought he would dry me off, put me down, but no. Neither.

He swung me completely up into his arms, carried me to the other room where a table was set with food, and placed me in his lap. "I asked for several Earth dishes. I hope you like one of them."

"Earth dishes?" I squirmed in his arms, but his grip only tightened.

"The other Earth mates requested special programming of the S-Gen units, the machines that make our food." He added the last, obviously for my benefit. "I chose several items from your planet for you."

Curious, I inspected the offerings. There were a couple things I didn't recognize, things that must be from Atlan, but there was some sort of rice dish with vegetables and chicken, spaghetti with marinara, pickles—which made me grin—a peanut butter and jelly sandwich, and a steaming filet mignon with asparagus and loaded mashed potatoes. The whole thing was ridiculously too much food.

I opened my mouth to tell him so, but the hopeful look on his face stopped me cold. He had done this, mixed a PB&J and asparagus in an attempt to please me. "It's perfect. Thank you."

His smug grin was worth the little white lie. "You will eat now. Which do you prefer we try first?"

"We?"

He cupped my cheek in his hand and tilted my face up to his. "Yes. We. I am learning you, mate. I will eat what you eat. And you will try some mild Atlan dishes as well."

Weird. Cute. Hell, I didn't even know what to say to that. "Okay." I glanced over the options one more time. I was starving. "The filet."

He reached for a knife and fork and handed them to me. "Cut it into equal bites. But do not place a single morsel in your mouth."

"What?"

"Do it, mate. Do not make me spank you again for disobedience."

9

WHAT. THE. FUCK? I BLINKED RAPIDLY AS HE LOWERED THE blanket from my bare shoulders and turned me on his lap to face the table. My lower half was still covered, the soft fabric pooled at my hips, but he had pulled my legs open over his so that, although I was covered, my pussy was spread wide. Wet. Ready for him. But my top? Bare.

It was erotic. Naughty. I loved it.

For a moment, I froze, uncertain just how far he was going to take this. But his hands rested on my hips, unmoving, and I managed to get my act together despite the five-hundred-degree temperature coming off his body that was making me overheat. I pulled the plate with the filet close and began to do as he asked. Knife. Fork. Cut.

It seemed really strange to do so with my bare breasts exposed. My nipples hardened, either from the cool air or from the concept of eating naked.

God, I *really* wanted a bite of those mashed potatoes.

He lifted my hair to the side, baring my spine, which he kissed. Slowly. Up. Down. His teeth nipped at my shoulder as his hands wound around my waist, then up higher to cup my breasts. I gasped, the fork clattering to the plate when he rolled my sensitive nipples between his fingers, his mouth locked onto the delicate area where my neck curved to meet shoulder. My pussy clenched, wet heat flooding my body as I tried to remember what I was supposed to be doing.

"Rezzer," I gasped.

"Finish, mate. I am hungry." He didn't mean for food. Or did he? I had no idea.

With shaking hands, I did as he asked, cutting the meat into pieces. It was hard to do, cut while he played with my breasts, but I did. Finally, I was done and put the utensils down.

I held perfectly still. Waited for him to stop petting me long enough to notice.

I was squirming by the time he let go of my breasts with a soft growl. "Beautiful mate. So big. Full. Soft. I can't wait to taste them."

"I'm hungry." I stared down at the food. Distraction.

"As am I. Place your hands in your lap."

I did as he asked immediately, instinctively. Jeez, who was this woman inhabiting my body?

When he turned me in his lap, laying me sideways like a pagan offering, I forgot to care. He lips closed over a nipple and the sound that left my throat was more animal than human. He suckled there, moving between them like he had all the time in the world. When I was panting, he lifted his head and lifted a bite of food to my mouth.

"What are you doing?" I asked, eyeing the fork.

"Taking care of my mate."

I blinked, coming up from the depths of erotic slumber. "I can feed myself. I'm not a child."

He simply stared. Waited. Confused, I opened my mouth and accepted the food. An explosion of spices and flavoring made me groan with pleasure. "God, that's so good."

He fed himself a bite, chewing slowly. Thoughtfully. For an impatient beast, his lack of hurry was killing me. "Rachel said it is a recipe from a famous chef on your world."

"Really?" So, not only did I not have to eat weird alien tentacles and bizarre bugs from other planets, but we had gourmet Earth recipes programmed into their system? "They should use that as a selling point for the Brides Program back home. You'd get more mates."

The curious tilt of his head was fascinating, as was his utterly serious tone. "I shall mention that to Lady Lindsey, Hunter Kiel's mate. She makes public relations videos for Warden Egara to recruit potential brides on Earth."

"What?" I was naked, aroused, being hand fed by an alien beast on another planet, talking about a public relations campaign on Earth? All this after I'd transported halfway across the galaxy and seduced said alien, who'd repeatedly said he wanted to give me to someone else. Then that he'd changed his mind.

No wonder I felt like my head was spinning, and I couldn't get my bearings. This was the weirdest day in the history of the world. And I'd had some doozies.

He lifted the fork to my mouth again, offering the bacon sprinkled, buttery, chive and sour cream smothered mashed potatoes. I promptly opened up and let him feed me.

Between bites, he played. His hands roamed beneath the blanket, tracing my inner thighs, teasing the wet heat of my core but never diving deep. Teasing and rolling my nipples. Kissing every inch of available skin. Torture.

Exquisite. Unrivaled. Torture. I never wanted it to stop. And if it didn't stop soon, I was going to lose my mind.

When I was full, I told him so, and he listened. Another mark in his favor. With a calm deliberation that made me nervous, he quickly finished off most of what was left, his hand stationed permanently low, over my womb, as if he could sense how badly I suddenly wanted a new life growing there.

I let my head loll back onto his shoulder and absorbed his strength, his warmth, the dominant yet protective hand on my lower stomach. His palm rested there, calmly, quietly, so possessive I fought back a sigh. I'd never been held like this. Fed. Pampered. Teased. I felt like the center of his universe, shocked to realize that, of all the men I'd dated over the years, not one had ever made me feel like this.

But then, if one of them had, I wouldn't be here, would I?

He shifted, moving more, but I ignored it until he lifted me with no warning.

Flailing, he quickly wrapped me back up and laid me down with my back on the table. A quick glance to the left and right showed that he'd somehow moved all the food. Well, almost all of it. A delicious looking slice of chocolate cake with caramel drizzle frosting was on one side of me, and an ooey-gooey slice of cherry cheesecake was on the other.

Umm. Dessert.

The way he towered over me, unwrapping me like I was his birthday present, made me all too aware that he definitely had plans for me—and all the sweets.

"Do you know what Maxim and Ryston told me about their sweet human female?" he asked, looking down at me with those green eyes, now dark with need.

"Rachel?" I whispered.

"Yes. Lady Rone." His hands dropped to my thighs, and he

spread my legs open, exposing my pussy to his eyes for the first time since we'd come to the table.

When I shook my head, he pulled his shirt off over his head, exposing his chiseled abs and huge chest. The silver flesh on his neck faded near his collarbone and halfway down his shoulder into smooth, sinful skin. God, he was perfect. Too perfect to be real.

"She loves something called chocolate. This cake in particular." He nodded toward the cake even as he stepped out of his pants.

How was I supposed to think about chocolate cake when he was standing between my legs, naked, his huge, hard cock just inches from my center?

Apparently, his patience was at an end, for he took two fingers, traced my wet slit and pushed them inside me slowly. The touch was shocking, sudden, but not unwelcome, and the walls of my pussy fluttered in welcome, drenching his fingers in wet heat. I was ready. More than ready. I'd been ready for half an hour.

"I feel my seed in you. Do you have any idea what that does to me?" he murmured in that dark, rough voice.

"Rezzer," I breathed.

His free hand moved to my breasts as he finger fucked me. But he kept talking. Damn it.

"But do you know what Tyran and Hunt told me about their sweet mate, Kristin?" When I didn't answer, he flicked my nipple, the sharp bite making me moan, and clench down even harder on his unmoving fingers.

"No."

His smile was great, but when he leaned over me and moved his fingers deeper, just a little faster, I gasped, my back arching up off the table as he devoured every nuance, every flicker of my eyes with complete devotion. "She prefers the red sweetness of this cherry cheesecake." He pushed his fingers deeper still, flicking my clit with his thumb as his face hovered directly over mine. He waited until I lifted my eyes to his. "Hands up, over your head, mate."

In. Out. His fingers pumped, working me open, making sure I felt his invasion. His heat was suffocating now. So hot. Too hot. If he didn't fuck me soon, I was going to melt on top of this stupid table. I couldn't breathe.

If someone asked me why, I wouldn't have been able to explain it to them, but I wanted to give him whatever he needed, whatever he wanted from me. I needed him to be happy. I wanted to please him, be exactly what he desired.

I lifted my arms over my head, and he reached up, quickly attaching them to something I'd not seen before. I was laid out, my cuffs linked and attached to something that held me down. Open. He waited again, watching me as if he had hours to take in the sight of my breasts pushed up by the position, my knees open and wide, my feet perched on the edge of the table. I was completely at his mercy.

"Which do you prefer, Caroline?"

"What?" What the hell was he talking about? I couldn't think. Not with his lips so close to mine, his body over me, his fingers pushing deep.

"Chocolate or cherry?"

God. Dessert. He was talking about dessert. "I like both."

That made him chuckle, and he dropped a quick kiss on my lips, just enough to make me want more. "Of course, you do."

He stood, pulled his fingers from my body and positioned the head of his cock there instead. Slowly, so slowly, he licked his fingers as he pressed his hips forward, pushing his huge cock inside me inch by intoxicating inch. I shifted, tried to take him faster, but he held my hips with his huge hands, locked me to the table. With my hands trapped over my head there was nothing I could do but take every massive inch. To open for him. To submit.

When his balls finally touched my bottom, my eyes were closed, tightly. And yet, I was seeing stars. Just the single, slick slide of his cock was going to make me come. So close. I was going to—

"No. You don't come until I tell you, mate." His hand landed on the inside of my thigh with a hot sting, and my eyes fluttered open. He was buried to the hilt, standing over me like a god, and he reached for the chocolate cake.

He pulled a small piece free with his fingers, heavy on the frosting and placed the offering right in front of my mouth. "Chocolate for my lady." His eyes were dark, intense. "Suck."

Wanting to give as good as I was getting, I lifted my head and sucked the delicious morsel into my mouth, finger and all. The chocolate was rich, dark, and the sweetly salted caramel was an explosion of decadence on my tongue. And beneath it all was him. Rezzer. My beast. And me. My wet heat. The erotic scent of my need for him.

It was the most erotic thing I'd ever experienced, sucking his finger until he groaned, until the huge cock filling me up twitched and seemed to grow even larger inside me.

"You are impossible to resist, mate."

He pulled back and thrust forward, the motion sending my breasts swaying and freeing his finger from my mouth. But I wasn't done with him yet. "I want the cherry cheesecake now."

Rezzer stepped closer, pulled my feet off the table and lifted my ankles to his shoulders. When he leaned forward to dip his finger into the cheesecake, he pressed my legs up and back, slamming deeper as he held the offering to my lips.

I devoured him, the sugary cherry syrup, the creamy, smooth taste of the cheesecake. And my mate. Mine.

Nothing had ever been this sexy. I'd never even heard of

anything like this from the trash-talking girlfriends back home. This wasn't just sex. This was…a reckoning. A claiming. Something so unique and intimate, I knew I'd never be able to sit at this table—or eat cake again—without remembering this moment. Ever.

This was Rezzer ruining me for any other, and I knew I'd never be the same again.

When I opened my lips and he pulled his finger free, he stayed low but pressed my thighs wide. I wrapped them around his waist and looked up into his eyes. "My turn," he said. "Feed me."

He reached over my head, releasing just one wrist so that I could do what he'd asked. I took a bit of chocolate cake in my fingers and raised it to his mouth. He sucked them clean, his cock buried deep, not moving. It was sensual. Strange. Exciting.

Using my inner muscles, I clamped down on his cock, a feeling of heady feminine power flooding me when he moaned. I was so wet, knowing it wasn't just my need that eased his way, but his cum from earlier.

"The cherry."

Twisting this time, I reached for the cheesecake and fed him again and clamped down on his cock. I teased him like he'd teased me as his tongue licked and sucked the sweets from my fingertips.

With a growl, he pulled my hand from his mouth and placed it above my head once more, locking me down. Leaning over me, he rested on his elbows, our noses nearly touching. "Who do you belong to, Caroline Jane of Earth?"

I wanted to be sassy, to deny him this, to save some part of myself for later, but it would have been a lie. The bath, his gentle feeding, his concern and control. He was perfect for me. I'd never felt this cared for, protected—loved—I'd never felt this loved in my life. Not from my parents, my siblings, ex-boyfriends. No one had ever made me feel like this. "You, Rezzer. You're mine. I'm claiming you, and I'm not giving you up."

He kissed me then, urgent and hungry, as if he were starving for my taste. His hips though, moved slow. Calm. Steady. Not enough. I needed more.

He bottomed out inside me and lowered his head to my nipples, sucking one strongly, then the other. He used his hand to hold the offering to his mouth, as if he wanted to swallow me down.

"Rezzer."

"Yes, mate?"

"Go faster."

He chuckled, and bit my nipple gently. "No."

I wiggled my hips. "No?"

"No. You are mine. I wish to take my fill of you. Enjoy your body."

"But—no. Please. I need more." I wasn't beyond begging now.

He abandoned one nipple, moved to the other, smeared chocolate frosting over the hard tip and suckled until it was gone. Cherry on the opposite breast. Driving me to madness. His thrusts not changing pace. "I know what you need, mate."

I tried to use my legs since he'd lowered them, the leverage I had with my ankles wrapped around his hips, but one shift, one huge hand on my abdomen, and I was well and truly glued to the table. "You're supposed to be a beast. Have some kind of mating fever. A beast, Rezzer. You're supposed to go crazy, lose control. Please—*lose control.*" I was truly begging now. Sad, but true. If he didn't fuck my brains out soon, I was going to have a stroke.

He shook his head and kissed me on the lips, a soft, lingering kiss. A merging of souls. "On the contrary, Caroline, a beast has ultimate control. I will never lose it, not with you. If I lost control, even for a moment, I would hurt you. Hurt others. While I was wild for you earlier, the beast had just been revived, not dangerous. We never truly let go unless it's too late for us, unless our fever strikes and our mate never appears."

"But I thought—" I didn't finish the sentence for he pulled out fast and fucked me harder. Deep. I shuddered, my hands clenched into fists above my head, my legs trembling so badly I had to lower them to the table because I could no longer hold them up.

"You are everything, mate. Your trust is everything. I will take care of you. Nothing is more important to me than you, not even my own life. I will never lose control." He moved faster, his body pressing mine down into the table until I could barely breathe. "But you will."

It was the beast looking out at me from those green eyes. He wasn't fully transformed, but his beast was there, just below the surface. Waiting. Watching. Just as hungry for me as the man.

He fucked me for several minutes then pulled out and smeared chocolate on my clit and over my swollen folds.

I was losing control before his mouth clamped down. Hard. He sucked me into his mouth without apology or hesitation, sliding three fingers inside as he made me scream his name.

Before the shockwaves were out of my system, his cock was back, spreading me open once more, my swollen body too tight. Too sensitive.

"Come, mate. Come again."

I came again as he filled me, unable to hold back.

My cries pushed him and the beast came out to play. He grew over me, inside me, his cock stretching me so tight I nearly came again from the erotic sight of the giant standing over me, fucking me. Filling me. Claiming me. I yanked at the cuffs, desperate to touch him, to hold onto something when I felt like my entire being was floating away. He must have sensed the need, because he blanketed me with his chest, grounding me in reality, in his heat, his scent, his strength so that I felt safe even though I was breaking apart, splintering into a thousand pieces and losing myself in the storm that raged in my body.

He didn't stop, but he no longer held back, his beast fucking me hard and fast, the sound of it filling the room along with our ragged breathing, my moans of pleasure, rocking his body against mine until we both shattered. I milked him of his seed, hungry for it, eager to take his life into my body and share that gift with him. A baby. I wanted *his* baby. To snuggle and kiss and protect.

He made me lose control. I couldn't deny it. But he also made me dream, and that was the biggest gift he could have given me.

ezzer, Zakar Private Quarters

"Excellent job," I said, walking up between my friends and slapping them both on the shoulder.

Tyran and Hunt didn't look away from their mate or their new baby as we came in. In fact, if the Hive came through the door, I doubted they'd notice. Although the way they eyed their loved ones with such possession, I had no doubt they'd defend them to the death.

Lady Zakar, their mate, laughed from where she was propped up in bed. She wore a white gown that covered her modestly, and the blankets were tucked about her waist. Kristin of Earth held her newborn baby in her arms, swaddled in a soft wrap. "Thanks, Rezzer, but I did all the work," she grumbled, but a smile played at her lips.

I knew her well, having worked beside her, hunted next to her in the caves below this world. She had been trained to enforce the law on her world, and that need had come with her to this one.

Her mates did not approve, but as I was discovering on my own, our mates from Earth were fiery and stubborn.

Kristin looked nothing like my mate with her short, blonde hair. She was smaller, too, of similar size to Lady Rone. Caroline had called herself an Amazon, although I didn't know what it meant, only that she was perfectly sized for me.

Finally, Kristin looked up from the babe in her arms but ignored me, only having interest in Caroline. "I'm so glad we finally get to meet. I'm Kristin, although everyone else calls me Lady Zakar."

"Yes, Hunt. Tyran. It seems we've kept our mates in bed for the past two weeks for completely different reasons," I said. I heard Caroline's little gasp before Lady Zakar frowned. I smiled as I clarified. "You were resting to ensure your baby's safe delivery, and I kept Caroline in bed to ensure I put a baby in her."

Caroline turned to me and swatted me on the arm. "Rezzer," she complained.

Lady Zakar laughed. "Come sit with me, Caroline. He's just being normal. All mates are possessive and proud of their virility."

Tyran walked over to the bed, leaned down and kissed the top of Lady Zakar's head. "And look what our virility made, mate," he said, eyeing his sleeping daughter.

"You're in big trouble now," Caroline said as she sat on the edge of the bed. "A girl. She's going to have you two wrapped around her little finger before she can walk."

Hunt made a grunting sound. "She already has. She will not be mated until she is thirty-two and they will live with us. In separate rooms," he added.

I didn't say a word, for I knew I would be just as possessive when it was my turn. The thought of Caroline holding our baby as Lady Zakar did, a cap of black hair on a little girl's head, a babe who looked just like my mate, made my heart swell and my beast pace and preen in equal measure.

Especially now.

We'd done it, my beast and I. Caroline carried my child. She didn't know it yet, but the signs were there. Over the past two weeks since she'd transported to The Colony and become mine, I'd learned her body well. Every curve. Every line. Her taste, her sounds of pleasure, the way she tightened before she came. The feel of her pussy after it had been well claimed, my seed slipping from her. Of course, I took to using my hand to slide it all back into her, making her come once more on my fingers to ensure the seed was pulled deeply inside her body.

I couldn't take my eyes from her. Everything about her hypnotized me. The soft sheen of her skin. Her smile. The graceful and feminine way she moved. The curves of her breasts and belly and hips. She was everything I'd never known I'd missed. My heart had been empty, but now it was filled. I'd had no idea it could grow to be bigger than my beast, and larger still with the potential for a baby. Something we made together. Something so perfect it was hard to believe it could be real.

Seeing Lady Rone and Lady Zakar heavy with child, playing with Kiel's new son, Wyatt, had awakened a need in me just as strong as the beast. Perhaps more so. More primitive. I'd been obsessed with planting my seed in my mate and taking her body whenever I wanted and anytime she needed. We were both voracious for each other. Insatiable. I'd thought my cock would be too much for her, that she'd be sore, but no. She'd awoken me in the night, sliding onto my cock, taking what belonged to her.

Not to be outdone, I'd roused her with my head between her thighs, tasting our mingled flavors.

That had been several hours ago and yet, my cock pressed against my pants with the want of her again, even as we stood, guests in the Zakar family's private quarters.

I took a deep breath, cooled my ardor until I could get her alone. Somewhere. Anywhere I could push up her dress and fill her. Oh, the seed had already taken, but just knowing there was a baby growing within her made me want her all the more.

The changes were subtle: her breasts larger. Heavier. Her nipples were darker and more sensitive; I could bring her to climax just from my mouth and fingers on them.

And lower, while her belly was still flat, she was always dripping for me, her inner folds swollen and sensitive. Aroused in a way she called horny. She was horny *all the time.*

I grinned, and Tyran pulled me in for a surprise hug. "It'll be your turn sometime soon."

Stunned by the overly affectionate gesture, I realized I would be behaving like him and his second in a matter of months. While this baby was the first born on The Colony, it seemed she would be the first of many.

"Ignore them. They're happy now. But you should have seen them during the delivery." Lady Zakar rolled her eyes, but there was laughter behind the gesture. And love. It shone from her like a beacon for every unmated male on The Colony.

Hunt's face went grim. "That was terrible. I vowed then never to fuck you again if it meant keeping you from such pain."

Kristin rolled her eyes. "And look what the pain brought."

She glanced down at the baby, who's tiny hand came out of the swaddling and curled into a fist. "Besides, it wasn't that bad. Not with all your medical gadgets and the ReGen wands." She looked up at Caroline. "Seriously, it's amazing. I had the baby, they put me in the ReGen pod for like, an hour, and I'm already healed." Her gaze drifted to her mates. "So, we'll see how long your ideas about leaving me alone last."

Hunt narrowed his eyes at her, but said nothing. She was right, and everyone in the room knew it was only a matter of time before her mates could no longer resist touching her. Relearning her body. Thanking her for the miracle she'd just given all of us.

"You have two mates," Caroline stated. "I've met Rachel and hers, but it is still so new to me. I have enough to handle with Rezzer and his beast." She looked up at me and winked.

"Enough?" I countered. "Am I too much for you, mate? You weren't complaining earlier. I believe your words were, 'more, more.'"

Even after all the things we'd done, my mate blushed.

The baby cooed and we all stepped closer. "She is well?" I asked.

"Perfect," Tyran replied proudly. "Ten fingers, ten toes. Looks just like her mother."

"We have been distracted by the impending birth and delivery," Tyran said, walking away from the bed and his mate. "I have not heard any news of Krael."

Caroline leaned in and brushed her hand over the baby's head as the women talked, Lady Zakar speaking of the delivery.

I joined Tyran at the edge of the room, leaned in and spoke quietly. "There is no news, although there have been daily sweeps of the caves." Krael was a known traitor, and we'd been hunting him for weeks. He was working with the

Hive, for what reason we had yet to understand. But his reasoning didn't matter. Not to me. I would see him dead for the harm he'd caused. Captain Brooks' death was just the beginning.

"The teams have been larger since your capture, I hear."

I ground my back teeth together. "Yes. The lesson was learned from me. No groups smaller than six warriors now search the caves. Eight to twelve is preferred."

I'd followed Krael in alone, being captured by his group of Hive hidden there. It had been stupid of me to do so, but if I'd had a teammate with me, he'd have been captured as well. I'd escaped after two days of tests and torture, but not unscathed. Whatever they'd been trying to do to me had cost me my beast. Until Caroline.

"Yes, but remember. If you hadn't been captured again, you would not have met your mate."

I looked over my shoulder at Caroline, who now held the baby. My beast practically howled at the sight. Her face was loving and soft in a way I'd never seen before as she spoke to the little one in her arms. She was more beautiful than I'd ever seen her. I grabbed my cock, shifted it in my pants.

"True. I cannot find it in my heart to regret it." I cleared my throat, my gaze wandering over the fullness of my mate's breasts under the Atlan gown. They were large, and now swollen as our child took root within her. The need to taste her nipples, bury myself deep and mark her and the unborn child as mine roared through my blood until I could barely hear Tyran's words.

I did not want to talk about the Hive or my torture at their hands. Not now. I needed something else entirely. "I will take my mate and allow you your privacy again." I nodded my head in deference to the new father, even though we were equals in rank.

"You want *your* privacy," he countered with a knowing grin.

I smiled back, or rather, my beast did. I struggled to keep him down as we were both eager for Caroline.

"Exactly." I strode over to the bed, and she looked up at me with such a beautiful smile, my breath caught. The baby was beautiful and precious, and even I knew she was not ours, but the scene was perfect.

Caroline lifted the small bundle to me, and I shook my head. The child was too small. Too fragile.

"Hold her."

Seeing the determination in her eyes, and not wanting to make her think I would fail in my role as father and protector, I held out my hands, shocked to see them trembling. I'd faced Hive Scouts and Soldiers, blood and chaos and killing, and not been this unsettled.

Smiling softly, Caroline placed the little one in my hands, the baby's entire body not filling them. So small. So sweet. So fragile and beautiful and perfect. I held the babe as if she were made of spun glass.

"Get a grip, Rezz. She's not going to break," Kristin pointed out from the bed. Caroline was too busy leaning up on her tiptoes to place a kiss on my cheek. Why holding an infant earned me such a gift, I did not understand, but the gesture brought me to my knees. I was in love with my mate. Totally and completely under her spell. There was nothing I would not give her. Nothing I would not do for her. No one I would not kill to protect her.

The baby made a strange gurgling noise and drew me from my musing. The child blinked up at me with huge, innocent eyes, and I could not help but stare back at her. "Hello, little one."

Caroline's hand came to rest on my arm as she peeked at the little girl. Standing together, like this, surrounded by family and hope and such miraculous innocence, something inside me shifted, healed. Became softer.

This is what I had fought for. This moment for billions of families on hundreds of planets. If even one father experienced such a blessing, all the pain and blood, the torture and sacrifice had been worth it.

Caroline watched me and wiped a tear from her eye. "God, you're so damn cute holding her."

Kristin laughed from where she watched us, propped against a sea of pillows. "Never thought I'd say this, Rezz, but she's right. Totally cute."

Cute? I could tolerate such blasphemy from my mate, but from Kristin, a member of the security team who worked with me? Hunted with me? No. I was an Atlan Warlord. A beast. I was *not* cute.

I lifted a brow and looked at my mate. But she wasn't looking at me any longer, she was looking at the baby with longing in her eyes.

"Someday, Rezzer. Someday, I will give you a baby."

Kristin groaned from the bed, taking her time as her gaze wandered up and down my frame. "Good luck, girlfriend. I thought a Prillon baby was big. I can't imagine an Atlan. But then, you're at least six foot. So much more room." She was rubbing her abdomen, but she was smiling. "I hate tall people. It's completely unfair."

Kristin sighed, the sound odd, but Caroline seemed to understand because she was grinning like the two women had shared some kind of secret.

"Six-one when I have to admit it." Caroline recited the numbers as if they meant something. I'd have to ask her to explain later as the words did not please the other female.

"God, I knew it. It's so not fair." The new mother was studying my mate with a look I knew well from our days in the field together, hunting Hive. "What did you do back on

Earth anyway? Rachel was a scientist for some massive pharmaceutical company. I was in the FBI."

"No way."

"Way." Kristin adjusted the blanket around her thighs and tried to reach for one of the pillows.

She struggled with it, and before I could blink, Tyran was there. She smiled at him with a softness I had not seen before. I knew her with an ion blaster in her hand, ready to hunt. This new version of her, soft and submissive, loving, was completely foreign. "And Lindsey is a public relations or journalist or something. She's making videos and handles The Colony marketing campaign back on Earth."

"I saw them." My mate confirmed. "She's really good."

"I know, right?"

Kristin settled back into her newly adjusted pillows as I held the baby. She'd fallen asleep, and I found I couldn't stop staring at her tiny little features, a mixture of Earth and Prillon warrior. She had her mother's softer features, but a golden tone to her skin that was lovely. Hunt and Tyran were going to need an arsenal to protect her from interested males. Gods, what if our child was female? I needed to begin gathering weapons now...

"So?" Kristin prompted.

"So what?" Caroline asked.

"What did you do? Back on Earth?"

"I was a market analyst on Wall Street. A broker. I was getting ready to open my own firm."

"What happened?"

"Convicted of insider trading."

"Did you do it?" Kristin asked.

Caroline chuckled. "Me and Martha Stewart." Her gaze slid to me, then back to Kristin. "This sounded like a better option than prison, plus all the fees, and I lost my license."

I had not heard any of this, but then I had not asked. I did not know what Wall Street was, or this style of trading my mate discussed. But Kristin understood, and she seemed unaffected by the revelations.

"So, you're an analyst."

Caroline shrugged. "I'm good with patterns and money. Great with financial statements and seeing through bullshit numbers."

"Excellent."

Hunt stepped forward, and I handed the babe to her father. Well, one of her fathers. With Kristin's genetic beauty on such display, it was impossible to determine which of the Prillon warriors had sired her. And I had been told that her mates preferred it that way.

"You can help the acquisitions and new arrival teams. With the new mates arriving here and on the other bases, and an increase in the number of contaminated warriors we are receiving, we could use someone with your skills to help us anticipate and determine what supplies and personnel to request from the Fleet."

Tyran stepped forward and lifted the baby from Hunt's grasp with a hungry look in his eyes that Hunt appeared unwilling to deny. "Yes, Lady Caroline. Hunt here could use your help. The whole base could use your help. Governor Rone is also setting up new defense perimeters, and we'll need to figure out how to supply the warriors out on patrol as well as create a schedule for payment and deliveries to the Fleet with so many of our warriors spending more time on patrol."

"Payment? What do you all pay with? I thought you were all dependent on the Fleet. That everything was generated by the S-Gen modules and no one paid for anything out here."

Hunt shook his head. "No. We don't pay with any type of money you would recognize. But we have the largest supply of the minerals necessary to run our transport technology. It was the reason the Prillon Prime decided to place The Colony here, on this ugly, forgotten world. We don't pay for anything, but we do have production quotas that need to be met."

"You're miners?" Caroline's gasp was outraged. "They banish you and turn you into miners?"

I placed my hand at the small of her back, unwilling to see her upset. "Not here, on Base 3. We are the operations center for The Colony. But on the other bases, yes. Some of the bases here are subterranean. The warriors live below ground so they can protect Fleet resources."

Kristin closed her eyes and leaned back with a sigh. "It's the reason we think the Hive are really here. If the Fleet loses this planet, and the natural resources here, the entire transport system would be crippled for weeks. Long enough for the Hive to—"

She didn't finish the statement, and I was glad. We all knew what was at stake, how badly I'd failed my people by not catching Krael and the Hive in the tunnels beneath the planet.

Tyran, however, just couldn't let it go. "Long enough for the Hive to take down the entire Fleet. If they take The Colony, they win the war."

Caroline's jaw tightened, and I saw a look I knew very, very well. Stubborn. Fierce. "I'm in. I'll help. Just tell me where to go and what you need me to do."

I pushed my mate toward the door, eager to have this discussion of Hive and my failures over. I would remedy my mistakes. I would go back into those tunnels. Krael would die. The Colony would once again be secure.

The door slid open and Kristin yelled farewell. "We'll set it up!"

"Okay!" Caroline twisted around me and tried to yell over my shoulder as the door slid closed behind us. I was happy to see her focused on a goal. My mate was intelligent and dedicated. I knew The Colony would not waste her talents, and I knew she would need something here, something to make her feel useful and important, a part of the community. But that would come. Another day. Right now, she was mine.

"Come, mate. We have an appointment."

11

"Rezzer," I moaned, my hands tangled in his dark hair. I was leaning against the exam table in the medical unit, Rezzer on his knees before me. He'd grabbed the hem of my dress and lifted it up so he could cup my breasts. Since I was bare beneath—he didn't give me any underwear, and I wondered if the lack was his doing, or if there really wasn't any in space—his mouth was on me, his tongue laving my clit as he tugged at my nipples.

"The doctor's going to come in."

He only growled as a reply, applying himself with a little more vigor to his actions.

I was close to coming. It didn't take much these days. I was so sensitive, so in tune to whatever Rezzer did. He was *that* good.

"Oh shit, I'm going to come."

He growled again and tugged on my nipples a little harder.

I was glad for the table at my back, otherwise I would have been a puddle on the floor.

With ruthless precision, his tongue flicked my clit in such a way that pushed me over the brink. I bit my lip, stifling my usual screams. In our quarters, I didn't hold back, but I knew just beyond the closed exam room door was medical staff. Which made my mate all kinds of naughty.

So damn sexy.

I couldn't catch my breath as Rezzer stood, wiping his glistening mouth with the back of his hand.

"God, what was that?" I asked.

He grinned, twirled his finger in the air. "Turn around, mate."

I did as he said—just as I always did now—without even thinking.

"If I have to explain it to you, I haven't done a good enough job."

He still held the hem of my dress in his hand and I was uncovered from the waist down. With a hand on my back, he pressed me forward so I was bent over the exam table. With his foot, he nudged mine apart.

I heard the sound of his pants opening.

"Rezzer, I don't understand."

My brain was all muddled from the orgasm, and when I felt the hot tip of his cock at my entrance, my thoughts scattered.

"I'm going to fuck you."

He slid into me in one deep, slow stroke. After all the times he'd taken me, I still wasn't used to his girth, and there was a slight burn at being stretched so wide.

"You're so tight, mate. Your pussy's perfect."

"Why here?"

"Because you have a greedy pussy and needed my cock."

He pulled back, thrust deep.

What he said was true. I had needed him. God, he'd fucked me in bed when I woke up, and that had only been a few hours ago. I was addicted. His cock was like a damned drug.

"But the medical unit?" I asked as I gripped the table until my knuckles went white.

The wet sounds of our fucking filled the room. I could feel the material of his pants against my bottom, and I knew he'd only opened them enough to free his cock. The thought of him being fully dressed and literally servicing me had me close to coming again.

"The doctor needs to confirm something."

He fucked me with a steady rhythm as he placed one hand beside mine, leaned over me.

"What? Obviously, your beast is fine."

He kissed the side of my face, behind my ear, and I felt him smile. I could feel his cock swell inside me, felt him grow larger against my back.

"My beast is well and very happy deep in your tight, hot, wet pussy."

I whimpered. I loved his dirty talk.

"My beast is also pleased about the baby."

"What does...oh god." He pushed deep and my entire body shuddered. I wanted to tell him to go faster, to hurry, to make me come, but I knew my words would be wasted. He was in control, and that made me even more desperate to come. Hotter. I closed my eyes and tried to think about what he was saying. "What does Kristin's baby have to do with your beast and fucking me?"

He pulled back, settled just at my entrance so the wide crown stroked over my g-spot. "Our baby, mate. We're here so the doctor can confirm that you carry our child."

I looked over my shoulder at him with wide eyes, then he plunged deep. I couldn't take the pleasure, and my eyes fell closed, a cry escaping my lips as he grabbed the rounded globes of my ass and pulled them apart, opening me to his sight. I was sure he was watching his huge cock slide in and out of me. A low, rumbling growl made my pussy clamp down on him like a fist. So. Fucking. Sexy.

"Our baby?"

He leaned down, nipped my bare shoulder. I trembled, my pussy fluttering, so close to orgasm, stretched wide around his cock.

"Ah, mate, you are so smart, yet it seems you do not know your own body as well as I do."

"You mean—"

"All this fucking, all this seed." He swelled in me, thrust deep, then filled me with more. "Load after load, it was all for you," he groaned. "All for that fertile womb of yours. We made a baby."

I couldn't think beyond how close I was to coming. He'd come, yet was still hard. His hand came around, found my clit, brushed it gently.

"Your sensitive breasts, your insatiable need for my cock, your ability to come with the slightest of touches."

He rubbed my clit, rough, fast, and I came apart in his arms, all over his cock, his free hand sliding over my mouth to stifle my scream.

"That's it. Come for me. Come for your mate. So good. Yes. I can't wait to see you round with what we made. To see you holding the infant we made. You're giving me everything my heart desires."

He kissed my neck as he praised me, as I came back to myself.

Only when I stopped pulsing and squeezing his cock, did he pull out.

"Ah, I love that sight. No need to work it back in, now, is there?" he asked as he pulled me up, let my dress fall back to hang long to my ankles.

I was unsteady, and he held me in his arms, the warmth of him seeping into me. His hands stroked down my back as I absorbed his words. Felt his seed slipping from me and down my thighs.

He had taken me so many times over the last two weeks that I'd lost count. He did have way too much cum for one man. But he was an Atlan and huge, so maybe it went with his size. My breasts did hurt, but I'd thought it was from Rezzer's constant attentions. And my period, it hadn't come. But I'd only been here two weeks, surely not enough time for me to be late.

Then how did he know? So I asked him.

"I know."

He smiled smugly and cupped my breast through the dress. I gasped at the gentle touch.

"Oh, I know."

It seemed a little backward that the man knew first, but he definitely paid closer attention to my body than I did.

"Can you stand on your own?" he asked.

I rolled my eyes. "It was good, but not *that* good," I countered.

"Ah, mate, a challenge. When the doctor is done, I will take you back to our quarters and ensure that your legs don't work at all. You'll just have to keep them spread so I can have my way with you."

He grinned, pressed a kiss to the tip of my nose, then went to the door. It opened silently, and Rezzer stuck his head out and said, "Doctor, we're ready now."

I hastily smoothed any real or imagined wrinkles from my dress and had to hope the doctor had no intention of taking it off. God, if I had to put my feet up in stirrups and he saw the evidence of what we just did...

The doctor held up a wand and he smiled at me. Doctor Surnen was big, a Prillon warrior with their oddly golden coloring and sharper features, and like everyone here the Hive had left their mark on him. His left hand was completely silver, but his smile was genuine. "Don't worry. This won't hurt."

He waved it in the air for all of two seconds, then turned it off, the red light fading. It looked like a miniature light saber from *Star Wars* but the glow came from within, not on top.

"Congratulations. You are expecting."

"What?" My mouth fell open and Rezzer grinned. That was it? Just a few seconds waving around a little glowing stick?

Rezzer leaned down, pulled me to him and kissed me tenderly. "You see, I was right."

I wanted the doctor to be wrong just so Rezzer wouldn't gloat, but then I wouldn't be pregnant. And I wanted his baby with a ferocity that shocked me.

"I'm pregnant? Already?" I asked, a hitch in my voice, and the doctor nodded. "That's it? That's all the testing you need to do?"

The doctor offered me a smile, one that was just pleasant and not ecstatic like Rezzer's. "You are completely healthy, Lady Caroline. You are having a baby. Time will prove me right if you do not believe the test."

"Thank you, Doctor."

Rezzer led me out of the med unit and down the corridor. Wow. He was practically beaming. I'd never seen such a big smile on his face. He appeared a foot taller and not because of his beast. He was proud of his manliness. He'd knocked me up, and he was all but preening.

I was letting him guide me as I was too overwhelmed. I was pregnant. With a baby. With Rezzer's baby. That we made by having lots and lots of sex.

I was having a baby.

And he'd known.

He leaned down and murmured. "I'm not done with you, mate. Here's what I'm going to do to you first. I'm going to—"

"Warlord Rezzer," a voice said, cutting in.

The guy wore a uniform similar to Rezzer's and equally commanding, although he was much smaller. Not tiny, probably several inches taller than me. He had mocha skin and black hair shaved close to his head. He looked human, but instead of two normal eyeballs, both of his eyes were shiny, metallic silver.

"Apologies, but the governor has requested your presence in command."

"Now, Lieutenant Denzel? I need to celebrate with my mate."

"Yes, he mentioned you have a mate. Congratulations to you and Lady Caroline." He gave me a deferential bow. "Where are you from?"

English. Definitely human. But God, those eyes were freaking me out. And just that fast I understood what Rezzer had tried to explain to me. Just because this man *could* return to Earth, didn't mean it would be a happy life. I loved my people, my planet, but we were all still savages, fighting over religion and territory and who had sex with whom. Gay, straight, trans, Christian, Muslim, African, Asian, whatever. The list was endless.

But silver, cyborg eyes in a tall, battle-hardened black man who'd spent two years killing aliens in space?

People would freak.

"New York. You?"

"Atlanta."

On impulse, I grabbed him and pulled him to me for a quick hug. Someone else from home. Someone who probably hadn't been hugged in quite a while.

He held me tight for a few seconds before reluctantly letting me go. The mood was heavy, so I did what I did best. "Denzel? Really?"

His grin was worth it, even if his eyes were still startling. "My mother named me after her favorite actor."

I laughed, loving it. "Denzel Washington? Your mom had a crush on Denzel Washington?"

"You know it."

I looked up at Rezzer, who watched everything with a quiet calm I knew was deceptive. "Can we order movies out here in space?"

"Of course."

I clapped my hands together. "Great. We're doing a Denzel marathon."

The lieutenant chuckled. "I'm all in. Couple other guys will be too."

"How many of us are there?" I asked.

He shrugged. "Less than a twenty humans on the entire planet, and most of us are here, on Base 3. And that includes the women. We aren't as big as the other races. They don't want us in the mines. Slows down production."

I had no idea what to say about that. "So what do you do instead?"

Rezzer wrapped his arm around my waist and pulled me to his side in a show of blatant possession. "The Lieutenant is an excellent sniper. His cyborg enhanced vision allows him to see targets almost two miles away."

"Holy cow. Really?" I asked. Denzel nodded but shrugged it off.

"Not much to shoot at out here."

"Yet." Rezzer said, and both men grew tense. Happy Earthling reunion time was officially over.

"Governor Maxim said you would wish to know that the sensors in the cave picked up movement."

I felt Rezzer stiffen beside me. He glanced down at me. "Come. I will work through my list with you later."

I didn't know what was going on, but I knew it was important. After what they'd done to Rezzer, I wanted to meet one of the enemy, too. Punch his lights out for hurting my mate. Yes, I could be just as possessive and protective as my big alpha male. And now that I had a child to think about, nothing and no one was going to take my man from us.

The Earth Coalition fighter escorted us down the corridor, Rezzer at my side as we followed him to the governor's command room. As soon as the door opened, Governor Rone looked up from a map and graphics on some kind of screen imbedded in the table in front of him.

"Rezzer. Good. Marz and Kiel are on their way with the rest of the team."

"What team?" I asked.

Rezzer pulled me closer, his arm around my shoulders as the others filed in, their footsteps heavy. He introduced me to the men. "Marz. Trax. Kiel. Warlord Braun. This is Lady Caroline. My mate."

They bowed, which was awesome and intimidating at the same time. Kiel was the only one who looked totally human, but he didn't move like one. He was too quiet and had too much contained power in his body. None of them were small, the Prillon warriors, Trax and Marz, both at least six-six. Marz was fair, like a Nordic god, and he had a strange silver ring of flesh around his eye and the eye itself was…like liquid silver. Oddly beautiful. Not quite as hard to accept in an alien face rather than a human one. The Prillon Trax was much darker, like a black man back home, but his hair was a deep rusty brown, like cinnamon sprinkled on coffee. His eyes were amber ringed with bronze, like tiger-eye gems. They were large warriors, attractive and terrifying, but none compared to my mate and the other man, Warlord Braun, who I recognized as an Atlan. A beast. Like mine. "Hello everyone. I'm CJ."

They rumbled off greetings, but I could tell they were distracted by the reason for the summons. I, too, was curious. They gathered around the governor who had done something to make the map he'd been looking at hover in front of him like a hologram. The image looked like a series of worms twisted around one another in the air. But as the others spoke, I realized they were caves.

"The sensors depicted movement here." Governor Rone lifted his hand to an area of the tunnels that turned red when he touched it.

"That's close." The one called Marz said, but I already knew it was bad news by the way Rezzer's hand twisted in the back of my dress. I wasn't even sure if he was aware of the movement. This news had him upset.

"You'll leave immediately," Governor Rone added. "We need to double patrols on the south side of the base. But that's not going to be enough."

"We need to go back into the tunnels." The beast named Braun crossed his arms and I noticed just how many weapons were strapped to every available inch of the Coalition armor he wore. His hair was a very light brown, almost golden and the warm color matched the dark gold of his eyes. He was, next to my Rezzer, the sexiest man in the room.

Not that I was prejudiced in favor of Atlans. Nope. I'd deny it if asked.

They all wore the same form-fitting black armor. I was surrounded by a feast of man-candy. I knew the governor had a mate, the copper collar around his neck the Prillon version of wedding bands, but I wondered about the others. Either way, their mates, or future mates, were lucky women. Not one of the warriors was as gorgeous as my Rezzer, but still. Not bad. Not too bad at all.

I needed to talk to the Earth woman, Lindsey, the public relations specialist I'd yet to meet. Rezzer had been too busy knocking me up for me to do so before now. Maybe a "hot men from The Colony" calendar would get more brides here. If that kind of campaign could get donations for fire stations back home…

"I'll lead the team." Rezzer's rough growl pulled me back to the present.

The governor stood and turned to my mate, his gaze purposely focused on the cuffs around Rezzer's wrists. "Not possible, Rezzer. You'll monitor the team and coordinate from here."

"No." He was changing, the beast rising to the surface. I watched, fascinated. I hadn't been able to see this without his cock inside me—which meant I was too distracted to notice exactly what happened. His eyes grew brighter; his shoulders filled up somehow. His whole body expanded before my eyes. It was crazy and fascinating, and all I could think about was how amazing his huge cock felt when he fucked me. I wanted to climb up his body and taste every inch. I just… wanted. Yeah, I was a total goner.

I felt my pussy grow wet, and Rezzer stopped in his tracks, frozen, to turn and look down at me. "Kill Hive. Mate. Stay."

He held up his cuffs and looked at mine.

"He can't go with them unless you take off your cuffs, CJ." Rachel appeared from somewhere and came to stand next to her mate, using her big belly to get the hulking warriors to move out of her way.

I remembered the pain walking away from Rezzer that first day had caused, as if I'd been hit by a cattle prod in both my wrists. I so didn't want that to happen again, and I had no idea what that would do to the baby.

I didn't like the idea of him going into danger, but I knew he needed this. Needed to end it. I wasn't going to get closure on the insider trading fiasco. Ever. And that hadn't been any big deal in comparison to what the Hive had done to Rezzer. Twice. He needed to take those bad guys down, let his beast go wild on their asses.

"You should go, so why don't you just take off your cuffs?" I asked.

"No!" Rezzer's roar made me jump, and I reached for him automatically. He actually lifted me off my feet, cradling me like a small child against his chest. Sheesh, he really was huge when he went beast. So freaking sexy. Could he feel my nipples harden against his chest?

I lifted my hand to his face and caressed him, just so he'd feel me, know he was still mine. It worked, and I noticed the other warriors in the room settle back into more relaxed stances, drop their hands from their weapons.

Had they really thought he was going to lose control over the idea of taking off his cuffs? The idea was sobering.

Rachel rested her hands on her round stomach—she would bring another baby to The Colony soon—and tilted her head with a sad smile. "He can't remove them. If he does, you'll be free to choose another mate. Those cuffs are your mark of ownership, your claim. Taking them off means he won't belong to you any longer. He'll have no reason to control his beast."

Rezzer nodded, obviously thankful she said what he couldn't. Not with his beast raging.

"What?" I looked into Rezzer's green eyes. I knew the cuffs were important, that they shocked the hell out of me if we got more than about fifty paces away from one another, but— "I thought they were just for me. To keep me close to you. Won't they cause you pain if you leave them on?"

He nodded again.

"Yes," the governor answered for him. "But just enough to remind him that you are waiting for him. That he belongs to you. That he needs to maintain control."

I looked down at the matching cuffs we wore with newfound awe. So, I could take mine off, but he would rather be in pain than lose his connection to me? "My *mark of ownership?*"

"Yes." Rezzer's response made me realize I'd spoken the last thought aloud. "Rezz. Belong. You."

I saw the truth of those three words in his somber green eyes. He was mine in a way I couldn't even begin to understand.

"They're not human, CJ. It's hard to realize it, but they're not even close," Rachel offered. I remembered Warden Egara's words, that any mate I was matched to wouldn't be like any Earth guy.

"Okay." Still looking into my mate's eyes, I held up my cuffs. "You want to go hunt? Track down the Hive?"

"Hunt." He didn't look away from me; the word was a promise, and I realized he felt like he needed to do this to protect me, protect everyone on the planet. Protect the new life growing inside me.

"Okay. Put me down." He settled me gently on my feet, and I held out my wrists to him. I had no idea how to take the cuffs off. No seam. No latch. Nada. "Here. Take them off."

With a tenderness that was shocking from someone so large, he did, showing me the pattern to trace, the trick to unlocking them.

They dropped into his large palms, and he winced just for a moment as the sound of a small electrical jolt emanated from the cuffs around his wrists. "You sure about this? It won't hurt you?" I ignored everyone else in the room, but I didn't care. This was between me and him.

"Mine." He wasn't talking about the cuffs.

Well, that about summed it up. I smiled. I couldn't help it as I took the smaller cuffs from him. "Well, you're mine, too. So hurry up and do whatever you have to do and come back to me. You'll help me put them back on, and then we'll go through that list of yours." I pulled his head down for a kiss, just a quick touching of our lips, but I wanted to do it there, in front of everyone. It was my claim.

Rachel was at my elbow when I let him go. "Come on. We'll go pretend to eat something and not worry while they go do their thing."

I walked from the room and didn't look back, the heavy weight of the cuffs in my hand a promise. He'd be back. He had to be.

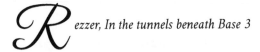

ezzer, In the tunnels beneath Base 3

WE ALL FOLLOWED KIEL THROUGH THE DARK TUNNELS. Strange alien worms lined the walls lending an eerie glow with their bioluminescence. We were deep underground, deeper than we'd ever been on these tracking missions before. But I did not doubt Hunter Kiel's, prowess. He had been methodical and efficient before meeting his mate, a human woman named Lindsey, and adopting her son as his own. But if he had been brutally efficient before, having a mate had not softened him. The opposite, in fact. Of all the warriors on The Colony, he would be the one I might struggle to defeat in battle.

Everian Hunters were fast. But Kiel was Elite, even among his own kind. He could move too quickly to track with the naked eye, and was nearly as strong as my beast when in hunting mode. Hunters were notorious throughout the Interstellar Fleet as bounty hunters and assassins. That Kiel was the only Hunter on The Colony had made him something of a legend. And when his mate had mysteriously appeared out of thin air, sent in a shipping crate by traitors from Earth, his legend had only grown.

The Hunters were notorious for being able to track their prey across solar systems on instinct alone. Some believed he'd used his abilities to magically lure a mate to him because she was here, and he hadn't even been tested by the Interstellar Brides Program. Superstitious nonsense, but Kiel did nothing to quell the rumors. I knew better.

He'd gotten lucky when Lindsey showed up here. Damn lucky.

"Report, Captain." The governor's voice came through all of our helmet communications systems. We remained silent waiting to see if Kiel deemed it safe to answer.

"Nothing so far, Governor," Kiel said. "But we're close. I can smell them."

I couldn't smell them, but every instinct I had was screaming at me that something was *wrong*. And my beast was holding on by a thread. The intermittent electric shocks blasting through the mating cuffs on my wrists helped keep me sane, helped remind me that my mate was waiting, that she needed me to finish this mission and return to her. Still, my hackles were up, my instincts roared through me. "Something's not right."

I was in the back, protecting our flank, and every second we lingered, my heart raced faster. The last time I'd been down here, I'd been captured. This wasn't a place I wanted to linger, but this time, I wasn't alone. Still, my gut was telling me—

"He's right. Something's not right, Kiel. I feel it, too." Captain Marz, the Prillon warrior, looked to Vance and they fanned out to my sides. We had come down in a team of eight, but divided in half about fifteen minutes earlier when the tunnel had split.

"Has the other team reported back in?" Kiel asked.

The governor's voice was hoarse. "No. But I need you to get Rezzer back to base."

My head snapped up, and I felt my eyes glaze as the beast fought for freedom. "Why?" It was less a question than a demand.

Maxim's voice came through clearly but did nothing to help calm my beast. "We need you back at Base 3, Rezzer. That's all I can tell you for now."

Something had happened to Caroline. It was the only explanation. He wouldn't pull me from a mission for anything less. And since he wasn't stating the reason through the comms, it was bad. "Tell me now, Maxim. Tell me now, or I'm going to rip the base to shreds looking for her."

"Control yourself, Rezzer." He didn't contradict my words about Caroline being missing. "Then get your ass back to base."

"We go back to base. Now." The change was right there, just under my skin, but I held onto control by my fingernails. For her. But when I met Kiel's gaze, he knew that if he didn't turn the team around right now, they'd be going on without me.

"Agreed," Kiel said. He nodded at Marz and Vance, and they began to walk toward me. Two steps later, all three of them had their ion blasters drawn and pointing at something behind me. I turned and saw what we'd spent the last three hours hunting.

Three Hive soldiers stood at the end of a long cavern, an offshoot we had yet to search. Unfortunately, they were just out of blaster range. Fuck. My beast snarled and grew.

"Hunter?" Marz asked Kiel for orders.

As the Elite Hunter on the team, Kiel was in command,

and as much as I wanted to go full beast, run down the hallway and rip those bastards to shreds, I had a mate to get back to. These assholes were so far down my priority list, they barely registered. As soon as Maxim indirectly told me there was something wrong with Caroline, they were nothing but in my way to get to her. Period. "Shoot them and let's go."

"They're out of range," Kiel said.

"We're not out of their range. Look at that rifle. What kind of weapon is that? I've never seen it before." Marz narrowed his eyes, and I knew his cyborg implant allowed him to see farther than the rest of us. "Take cover!" he shouted.

Too late. A sharp pain stabbed me on the left side of my chest, and I looked down to find an odd dart protruding from my uniform. With a growl, I reached up and plucked it from my flesh but a strange disc about the size of my fingernail remained attached in my uniform. "What the fuck?"

"Take cover!" Kiel was yelling now. He was on the ground, as were the other two.

I wasn't sure what was happening. The Hive could have killed me. They could have blasted my head off or poisoned me with that dart. But they'd done neither. I studied the object stuck to me, craning my neck to get a better look. The others stood and Marz came up on my left side, pulled my arm.

"Come on, Rezzer. Move it."

As soon as I started moving, he let me go and I followed him. I wanted as far away from these damn caves as possible. With each step I took, I was closer to Caroline. The pulsing pain from the cuffs was my reminder. We darted down a side tunnel. The moment we were out of their line of sight, we stopped and the other two gathered around me to inspect the object.

"Get that off your uniform. Now!" Even as he said it, Kiel took a step back. "Get it off. It's a remote transport beacon."

"What?" Marz looked shocked. "How the hell did the Hive get a transport beacon?"

Kiel rubbed his brow even as he kept his eye on the tunnel entrance. "A MedRec unit was hit a few weeks ago. Rogue 5 mercenaries took out an entire MedRec team with Battlegroup Zakar. Took hostages for the slave trade and stole the weapons and transport beacons."

"By the gods, Kiel. Why weren't we told?" Marz asked.

"It was need to know." Kiel shrugged his half-hearted attempt at an apology. "They never thought they'd sell to the fucking Hive. And I sure as fuck never thought they'd end up here."

"Right. With us. Contaminated," Vance added.

"They were wrong." I lifted my hand to the tiny device as both Marz and Vance stepped back. I didn't blame them. If this thing went off, I was quite sure they didn't want to go wherever the Hive would take me. Wherever the fuck it was programmed. The beacon was small, almost too small to grab with my large hands. And I wasn't quite sure I wanted to remove it. I had a feeling that this—combined with Maxim's communication from a few minutes ago—was all part of something larger at work. Something that had to do with Caroline. The Hive had aimed for me. Hit me with the dart. They were expert marksmen, not aiming at the four of us and randomly tagging me.

Kiel inched his way toward the opening and peeked around the corner to check on the status of the Hive soldiers we knew were following us. His confused expression confirmed my suspicions. "They're gone." Kiel stepped farther into the corridor and lifted his nose to scent the air. "Where the hell did they go?"

Marz followed him and used his cyborg vision to check the cave in both directions. "You're right, they're gone." Both men turned back to me.

"Get that fucking thing off." Kiel's eyes looked glazed, the closest I'd ever seen him to a panic.

I ignored his command and looked him dead in the eye. "You have a private communication channel with the governor?" It was standard operation procedure. The commander of a unit always had a way to talk to core command without alerting the others on the team.

His nod was so small it was nearly imperceptible.

"Tell me what he didn't want me to know." I allowed my beast into my voice, the deep growl rumbling through the small cave. I reached up to remove my helmet, the confines too tight when I was on the verge of changing into my beast.

Kiel took a deep breath and looked at me, the resignation in his gaze making my heart sink into my stomach like a heavy stone.

"Someone on the inside got to CJ. They used a transport beacon—" He pointed to my chest. "—just like that one."

"The Hive was inside Base 3?" Marz was practically shaking with rage. Base 3 was our home and we'd taken enough abuse from the Hive to last a lifetime. And I'd walked away, left her alone when there were fucking *Hive* to hurt her? My beast growled, the rumble heard by the others.

Kiel shook his head. "No. Not Hive. A medical transport worker. He was a medical officer from one of the shuttle teams. He's only been here a few weeks."

"So the Hive was controlling someone on the inside and they tagged her."

"She's no longer on The Colony," Kiel replied grimly.

"They kidnapped my mate?" Cold fury held me in check now. Raging like a beast would not do my mate any good, not now. She needed me like this, calm and calculating. "Did they track the transport signal?" The words were bit out, a snarl.

"They're working on it now. Maxim hoped they would have a location locked down before we returned."

The device on my shoulder began to hum, the vibration of energy more feeling than sound. But I knew what it meant. I glanced from the transport beacon to Kiel. "I can't wait. Tell him to hurry up and send reinforcements."

"What do you mean?" Vance asked, but stepped back with a curse as the energy of the beacon expanded. The hair on my body rose to attention, and they no doubt could feel the sizzle of the transport current in the air.

Marz stepped forward placed his hand on my shoulder. "I'll go with you."

"No. That won't work," Kiel said. "They can't transport both of you with one beacon. They're not designed that way. One warrior. That's it. If you don't let go of him, it might not work at all."

"Good," Vance said and grabbed my other shoulder.

"No." I shoved him away, hard. Broke the strong grip. I would have hit Marz as well, but he'd already stepped back, understanding in his gaze, so I didn't waste words on him. I turned to Vance. "This is going to take me to my mate. Touch me again and I will kill you."

"By the gods, Rezzer, you should wait for Maxim to assemble a ReCon team," Kiel insisted.

The beast growled before I could stop him, and I fought to keep my voice under control. "And if the Hive had your mate, or your son?"

I'd won, I knew it by the way Kiel's shoulders slumped, his gaze fierce. If it were his mate, Lindsey, who had been taken, or his son, Wyatt? Nothing would stop him from getting to them. Nothing.

The buzzing filled my ears until I wasn't sure they would hear me, wasn't even sure that I spoke. "This will take me to Caroline. I know it. They targeted me. Took her. We're exactly what they're after. Tell Maxim to bring a fucking army. He can have what's left of the Hive when he gets there."

Kiel tossed me his weapon so I had two. I gave him a nod of thanks, then crouched down on one knee and stabilized myself on the ground as the transport beacon took me. I had no idea where I was going, but I would destroy anything and anyone between me and my mate.

13

I RUBBED MY FACE OVER THE SOFT PILLOW AND TOOK A DEEP breath. Rezzer. It smelled like my mate, and I snuggled down in complete bliss. My eyes popped open when I heard a ringing. At first, I thought the sound was my cell phone, but the tone was different. Rolling over, I opened my eyes and blinked at the now familiar lines in the ceiling of our private quarters. The room had started out utilitarian. Useful, but not comfy. Not warm.

I'd been adding little touches since moving in. A soft, fuzzy green blanket and matching pillows on the couch. Lamps with antique looking shades on two new end tables so we didn't have to sit in the stark, standard, bright white lighting provided by the Fleet. I'd even asked Rachel to help me with the S-Gen machine and magically made cinnamon cookie scented candles—which had to override the computer safety protocols to burn—and a large, red-leafed plant the strange alien in charge of their gardens had recommended when I told him about my black thumb. I had to hope it was kill-proof. Our place wasn't exactly going to win any awards for interior decorating, but at least it felt like a home now and not a barracks. A real home. Ours.

And soon we'd be moving to a bigger suite, one with another room. A room I couldn't wait to decorate for the baby. I smiled to myself at the thought.

The ringing sounded again, and I groaned. Moving too quickly, I was swamped by dizziness and nausea. Lying back down, I took a deep breath and fought not to panic as my brain kicked in. I hated being sick. No, I wasn't sick, I was pregnant now. With an alien baby.

Maybe I'd have to get used to not moving quite so fast…

Seemed that if the Coalition scientists could eliminate the need for cell phones, and implanted everyone with an elaborate NPU, Neural-Processing-Unit—the fancy gadget imbedded in my skull that acted like a universal translator—they could figure out a way to get rid of morning sickness. I'd have to talk to Kristin and Rachel about it. They wouldn't stand for throwing up if the doctor had a way to avoid it.

Every once in a while, my head ached from the NPU. But I understood every language in existence. That was technologically cool, but being connected to an alien computer system that had matched me to my new mate was even more amazing. Rezz. My beast.

I missed him. We'd only been together a short time, but I found that I loved sleeping in his arms, loved waking up to his heated touch, loved that his beast liked to come out and play rough. I loved that he was big and virile and had no problem at all with a six-foot, smart-mouthed woman for a mate. He didn't call me an Amazon. He had no idea what the term even meant. To him, I was small. The more I sassed, the more orgasms I seemed to get. The more I denied his dominance, the more he asserted it. In bed. Out of bed. Up against the wall. Naked. Dressed.

I squirmed beneath the sheets, wishing he were with me now. Maybe, just maybe I'd let him take control. Yeah, right. As if he'd have it any other way.

Really, the beast had zero limits and absolute, unbreakable control when he took me so skillfully, making me scream with pleasure.

He hadn't figured out my diabolical, orgasm-producing scheme yet, or at least he pretended not to know what I was doing. Which was even better. I closed my eyes and smiled once more as the room stopped spinning. My pussy was a little sore—in a good way—and I was sticky there with his very potent seed. He was virile, and wild, and he'd worn me out. That, combined with the news that I was carrying a baby had been all I could handle once he left with the others on his mission. I felt bare without his cuffs on my wrists—I hadn't realized how I'd become used to their heft, the cool feel of them until they were removed—but I knew he would come back to me.

For the first time in my life, I had absolutely no doubt that I was wanted. Needed. Loved. The feeling was both heady and addictive and probably why I'd fallen in love with my beast so hard and so fast. It was insane. I remembered the conversation with Warden Egara, how I'd insisted that I didn't have to *like* my mate. No wonder she'd practically rolled her eyes at me. I'd been stupid. Naïve.

I know how true love feels. What it can be between mates. Her words stuck, and I would have to call her on the comms unit, tell her she was right.

I opened my eyes, blinked away the sleep. This room already felt like home. It was safe. Ours. Instead of going to eat with Rachel, I'd come back here and fallen asleep within minutes of his leaving.

I'd tried to stay awake waiting for Rezzer, but obviously that hadn't happened. He hadn't returned, since his side of the bed was still made, and cold. I longed for him, but I was thankful I wasn't doubled over in pain from the separation. It had *hurt* that one time the mating cuffs had shocked me, and I had no interest in experiencing that again. But I also longed to put them back on. I'd adjusted to wearing them, and after seeing the intensity in Rezzer's gaze when he refused to remove his, I learned their value.

They weren't just bracelets. They were a sign, proof, of so much more. He wore my claim still, choosing to endure the pain from the cuffs rather than be separated from me even in that. It was humbling, and worrisome that I held so much influence over such a powerful being as an Atlan Warlord. Exhilarating and frightening and sobering.

Would the constant shocks from the cuffs distract him? Put him in danger? I shook off that thought, knowing Rezzer was a Warlord. Skilled at fighting. He wouldn't do anything stupid.

Yet the cuffs were also proof of just how vulnerable he was. His beast was strong. Terrifying to his enemies.

And lost without me.

I put my hand on my belly, thinking of the baby within. Our baby. I wanted Rezzer safe, here in bed with me. If something happened to him, well, he wasn't the only one with an inner beast, and mine was going to rage.

A ringing came again.

"Hello?" I looked around the room, realized the sound was coming from a doorbell of some kind.

"Hello? Is someone there?" I padded across the room on bare feet, the wrinkled dress I'd been wearing all day embarrassing, but not the end of the world.

Ring. Ring.

Pushing my hair back from my face, I froze when a door

opened without my permission, a piece of the wall sliding away and disappearing. A medical officer—I was now familiar with the green uniform—bowed to me. He wasn't Prillon or Atlan. I recognized him. But from where?

"Lady Caroline. Congratulations on conceiving with your Atlan mate."

"Thank you. We are very excited." I offered him a small smile. "I know you, don't I? Where are you from?" He wasn't Atlan. Not tall enough. He wasn't Prillon. Didn't have the coloring or the sharp facial features. He didn't move like Kiel, who I learned was from Everis. I wasn't sure what other planets were represented on The Colony, but this guy's origin was a new one for me.

"Trion. And no, we have not formally been introduced."

Well, I'd never heard of Trion. But whatever. He looked almost human, closest alien race to human I'd seen since stepping foot on Base 3. There were well over two hundred worlds in the Interstellar Coalition, and I'd always been hopeless at geography. Adding that many more planets with new places and landmarks to my non-existent knowledge base just wasn't going to happen.

He stepped toward me, and I stepped back. I frowned. He was a little too close, and I felt like a kindergartener whining because he stepped into my "bubble". The look on his face wasn't threatening...but it wasn't friendly either. A chill raced over my skin as the door slid shut automatically behind him. We were alone. Together.

"Why are you here? Where is Rezzer? Has something happened to him?" I didn't like this. Didn't like the way he was looking at me like I was... No. Not looking *at* me. Looking *through* me. Like I wasn't even here. There was no empathy or acknowledgment in his gaze. It was like he was hypnotized. Or a robot.

"Your mate is fine."

Well, then? What the hell was this? I cleared my throat. "You need to go now. Rezzer will be back any minute."

His calm demeanor shifted, and all at once he was tense, his dark eyes hard. "It has been confirmed that you are with child." His voice was deep and menacing. Yet he appeared unarmed. No sexy thigh holster like Rezzer wore.

"Was that a question?" I stepped back again, not liking there was no one else around. The door was closed, providing a privacy I didn't want. No one knew he was here —at least that I knew of—and Rezzer wasn't around. And I had no idea who this guy was. What he wanted. Why he'd rung the dang doorbell in the first place. I stepped back far enough to wrap my hand around the thin neck of one of my new lamps. God, I hated to ruin it, but it was the only weapon I had. He was tall, but he was no beast. Had me by maybe six inches. I could swing the lamp at his head. Maybe kick him in the balls. No guy, alien or human, liked getting whacked in the nuts.

His gaze darted to my hand where it wrapped around the lamp, but he looked amused, not threatened.

Bastard.

Reaching into his pocket, he pulled out a small disk about the size of a round cracker, and my mind raced, ideas clicking in and out of place like puzzle pieces as adrenaline surged through my body. What was this alien doing here? What the heck was that little round thing? His smile was definitely *not* human, and he thought it was actually meant to *reassure* me? Yeah, right.

"Your mate is far from here, Lady Caroline. But do not worry, you are very valuable to us now. And he will be joining you soon."

Us? Who was *us*? And joining me? Why did that sound like a threat? Every instinct I had screamed at me that I was in deep shit, but there was nowhere to run. "I don't remember you from medical. I think it's time for you to go. As I said, Rezzer will be back any moment, and I assure you, he's very possessive. He's an Atlan, you know." I added the last to remind him that Rezzer turned into a beast and could rip his head off if he did anything to hurt me.

He shrugged his broad shoulders, clearly not threatened by being ruthlessly killed by an Atlan beast. "I only need a moment," he replied, stepping close. Too close.

I swung the lamp. Prayed for a miracle.

Fuck. He was stronger than he looked. He stopped my assault with one hand, and didn't even grunt. Didn't blink. His face never even changed expression. He was empty. Just…empty.

Still holding the lamp in one hand, he reached out and slapped the round disk onto my one bare shoulder. Only then did he step back, giving me the space I wanted. He didn't even take the lamp from my hand. Glancing down at the disk, I watched as a series of lights blinked yellow, the pattern looked like a…an electronic button.

"What—"

I reached up to pull the disk off my skin, but I felt a sizzle, every hair on my body standing up on end. Then it was like the world twisted me from the inside out. Painful. Strange. I tried to scream, but there was no air. Nothing to hold on to. Just…nothing.

CJ

I STUMBLED, PUTTING MY ARM OUT INSTINCTIVELY, AND IT slapped against a wall. I blinked, felt nauseated, realized I'd transported. When I had left Earth, the last thing I'd remembered was Warden Egara counting down and a calming blue light. I'd woken up on The Colony coifed and shaved and wearing a beautiful gown. And the best part? Rezzer had been there. Waiting. Watching me with those gorgeous green eyes.

This time, I hadn't slept through the travel and boy-oh-boy, the ride really was not enjoyable. It was not as fun as I'd thought it would be. *Star Trek* made it look so easy. I knew my ions or cells or whatever rearranged, and I went through some kind of vortex.

Oh god. The baby. Had it rearranged the baby? How many pregnant women transported? Was it allowed?

I put my hands on my belly, felt nothing. Of course I didn't. But I didn't feel like I was losing the baby either. No cramping or blood.

Glancing down at my dress, I expected to see the one I'd been wearing all day. Instead, I wore a simple white shift that fell to just below my knees. No shoes. No underwear. If it had been open in the back, it would have been exactly like a hospital gown back home. But the material was smooth, oddly unwrinkled—without the smallest crease—and seemed to have some kind of internal circuitry woven into the fabric. If I stared long enough, I saw small bursts of light, or electricity...hell, I had no idea what it was, but it looked like circuits bolting this way and that at seemingly random intervals.

Rubbing the fabric between two fingers, I braced myself on the wall and looked up again. I wasn't in our quarters. I wasn't anywhere I'd ever been before.

I was in some kind of personal quarters. The bed against one wall was large, just as big as the one I shared with Rezzer in our suite. A small table was affixed to the floor, the chairs bolted down too, and all three items were bright silver, like shiny chrome. There were no pictures, no other furniture. I peeked through a small archway and saw a bathing unit, sink and a small closet with additional gowns exactly like the one I wore.

No S-Gen unit. No decoration. No smell. Why didn't this place smell like *something*? I felt like I was inside a sterile bubble. No dirt, no plants, no hint of food or people or... anything. "Where the hell am I?"

My heart raced, and I had to fight to stay calm as the little circuit lights in my gown went crazy.

"If you are feeling poorly from transport, sit."

I spun about to see three men in the room. How the hell had I missed them? I gulped and put a hand on my heart to try to keep it from beating out of my chest. No, they weren't men...exactly. They looked nothing like men from Earth. They weren't any aliens I recognized either, nor were they the same as the guy who'd put the transport thingie on me.

Remembering it, I peeled it off my shoulder, wincing as it stuck to my skin. It was worse than a super-glued bandage on inch long hair. I was afraid it was going to take the top layer of my skin with it, but decided it was like a Band-Aid, and I ripped it off, hissing out a breath with the sting. I gripped it in my fist, thinking I might need it to get out of wherever I was. If it got me here, it could get me away.

The three stood next to a glass window about as tall as Rezzer but twice as long. No, not a window. More like a sliding door made out of one-way glass. I had a feeling whoever was on the other side could see me, but I couldn't see them. No natural light came through anywhere, and I had no idea if it was day or night, had no idea of the time. I could have been a mile underground or ten thousand miles out in space. I probably was. All I knew was that I didn't feel like I was on The Colony anymore.

"Come. You must recover from transport." The middle alien was slightly shorter than the other two, his skin a deep, matte blue that I'd never seen before outside of the sci-fi romance section of one of my favorite e-book series. He had a weird hook-like thing coming out of the back of his head that seemed to connect into his spine somehow. He was just…strange. But then, with so many worlds in the Fleet, and me having met a total of four or five of the alien races, I imagined there was a lot of strange out here in deep space that I had yet to see. Still, I wasn't really interested in learning about other alien races now. I wanted to be back in my quarters on The Colony. With Rezzer.

"Who are you? Where am I?" I asked.

"I am Nexus 4. A medical unit. Come. You are dizzy." He held out his blue hand to me, and even though I ignored it—he wasn't quite as automated as the Trion man who'd gotten me into this mess in the first place—I did walk closer to the glass, more from curiosity than anything else. None of them made any threatening moves. The situation had become almost dreamlike. Surreal.

I approached the glass, and they remained motionless as my reflection stared back at me in the smooth surface. When I placed my palm flat against it, it felt as cold as a car windshield during a New York winter. I yanked my hand back, the outline clear where the heat of my palm had caused a change in the surface.

Whatever I'd done must have worked because the glass slid to the side, and I gasped, wrapped my arms around my stomach and backed right into Nexus 4. His hands came down on my shoulders like iron fists, and my fear came roaring back full force as I stared at a medical exam room, complete with an exam table…and stirrups.

I shivered at the touch, cringed at what I was seeing. "No way. I'm not going in there."

"It is necessary to check on the health of the baby after transport." The alien on my right pointed to the exam table.

Clinical space with gray walls, gray floor. The lighting came from the ceiling but without any fixtures. If I weren't already in space, this room would make me believe in aliens.

So would the triplets surrounding me. Not triplets by birth, for they looked nothing alike. The one on the right had pale hair, yellow skin. The left guy had hair as dark as mine and a strong, square jaw. And then there was the blue alien who held my shoulders.

Different. But the one thing they all had in common were the Hive integrations I recognized from those I'd met on The Colony. But these three didn't have the odd patch of skin here, a silver eye there. No. At least a half of their exposed skin was covered with metal. Bionic parts. Eyes, ears, neck, hands. Artificial, looping spines.

"I'm fine," I murmured, but moved away from them. "The baby is fine." Since they were blocking my path, I was only moving farther into the room.

"We will determine the health of the child." The blue one seemed to be the leader of the triplets since he answered me. Again.

"Where am I?" I asked.

Silence.

"Why am I here?" I looked frantically from one to another, then back at the large blue creature standing almost protectively near me. The other two seemed to be under his control, which shouldn't have made me feel any better, but somehow, it did.

"Because you are having a Hive baby."

My gaze lifted to his, and the shock was like a hit of the best drug I could ever imagine taking. My mind just...stopped.

My hand remained on my belly out of instinct, although if these three wanted to do me harm, nothing was going to stop them. I had no weapons. Glancing around the room, there were no sharp objects, no way to hide and nothing to use as a shield.

"A...a Hive baby?" I asked, a laugh escaping. That was ridiculous.

The guy on the right went to a wall and retrieved a now familiar wand. When the red light came on, I knew it was the same one the doctor had used on The Colony to confirm I was pregnant.

"We will approach you now to confirm the baby survived transport."

My heart lurched at his harsh words. Did he think it—the *baby*—wouldn't? Oh god.

I nodded at him to proceed because I needed to know the answer. Otherwise, I wouldn't have let him near me, at least with my consent. I held perfectly still as the blue alien's minion stepped close and waved the wand over my abdomen.

Nexus 4 watched without blinking, his entire body covered in a dark silver and gray armor I'd never seen before. He wasn't quite as big as the other two, who I'd figured out were both Prillon warriors underneath all that silver skin and odd parts, but he stared, and I blinked. Hard. Tried to shake off a feeling of acceptance and well-being.

The longer I looked into Nexus 4's eyes, the more I forgot to be afraid. Forgot who I was. Why I should resist...

"Confirmed. The child survives intact."

Nexus 4 looked away from me when the other alien made his proclamation. I nearly sagged in relief at the knowledge that the baby was all right—and that he'd broken eye contact. Was he a hypnotist? God, what *was* Nexus 4? I glanced at the exam table. The stirrups. The strange glowing circuits in my hospital gown. "Is this a hospital? What are you going to do with me?"

Nexus 4 stood still as the other two walked into the exam

room space and out a door I hadn't noticed until now. "You will not be harmed, Lady Caroline, matched mate of Warlord Rezzer. We are going to do nothing but observe, run occasional tests, and make sure both you and the baby are healthy."

My mouth fell open. I was a prisoner, but protected. "What? You can't keep me here?"

"We can."

Now that just made me angry. I narrowed my eyes. "For how long?"

Nexus glanced at something on one of the data screens behind me as the other two returned. "For another two-hundred and sixty-four days. After that, you will be bred again."

My mouth fell open. "Bred again?" I pinched my lips together after those two words slipped out, the math kicking in. Two hundred and sixty-four days? That was roughly nine months.

"You want my baby." Now I really felt ill. No transport needed.

"We want nothing. The child is Hive. The child is ours." He blinked for the first time, a strange, nearly translucent film coming down to cover his eyes briefly before lifting again. "The baby will be the first Hive born, free of contamination."

I crossed my arms, suddenly cold. They wanted my baby? That was *not* okay. "Hive born? I'm human. The father is Atlan. There is no Hive."

Nexus 4 looked at me, and his eyes were eerily dark with no pupil, like a great white shark's. But when he held my gaze, I couldn't argue, couldn't move. Didn't want to. It was like I just...forgot who I was. One of the others moved, breaking his hold on me, and I fought my way back to our conversation. It was important. He was talking about my baby. "This baby is mine. It was nothing to do with the Hive."

The large blue alien tilted his head, looking at me as if I were a complete idiot. Nothing like being mansplained to by a freaking alien. "Your mate is Subject Zero. His physiology was altered so that his genetic offspring would be born free of contamination."

"What contamination? What are you talking about?" My hand drifted over my stomach like a shield. His complete lack of emotion was beginning to really, really creep me out. This was the Hive. *This was the enemy.* Destroyer of worlds. They annihilated complete planets, civilizations. They left nothing and no one behind once they conquered a world. So what the hell did they want with me? Or Rezzer? Or my baby?

"We do not recommend diverging information to the human." The dark haired former Prillon warrior spoke to Nexus 4 as if he were relaying a message.

Nexus 4 ignored him, his complete attention on me. "The Atlan race does not accept integration well."

A harsh laugh escaped me at his frustrated tone. A beast? Accept their implants and Hive mind mentality. "That's not surprising."

He continued. "Atlan Integration rate has less than a four percent survival rate."

I was shocked it was that high, knowing my mate like I did. "They fight you, don't they? Their beasts don't like your mind control. They don't follow orders."

He didn't quite nod, but it was close. "Subject Zero was altered on a genetic level to produce what we need."

"What did you do to him? To Rezzer?"

If Nexus 4 hadn't been an emotionless freak, I would have said he was preening. "We spliced his DNA with instructions for protein synthesis complementary to Hive biotechnology.

High levels of the new proteins cause cellular adaptation and evolution of the complete biological system. The suppression of his natural transformative process is central to our experiment."

What the hell did that mean? Suppression? As in, the reason he couldn't turn into his beast when I arrived on The Colony? This blue alien was talking way above my pay grade. I was a financial person. I'd barely passed tenth grade biology. "I don't understand what any of that means. What does it have to do with my baby?"

"Subject Zero's biological offspring will be born with the same genetic improvement."

"Improvement?" Oh, fuck. They genetically engineered my baby to be *complementary to Hive biotechnology*? To have his beast suppressed?

I took a step back as my stomach lurched. The little lights on my gown went crazy again as my pulse raced out of control. Was that why Rezzer couldn't turn into a beast? Because of their genetic splicing? Gene therapy? Proteins? My head hurt, and nothing he said made sense. But their trick didn't last. Rezzer's beast was back. Did they know their DNA thing didn't work on Rezzer? Did that mean my baby was Hive or not?

I was going to vomit. Apparently, Nexus 4 was on a roll, for he kept talking.

"The new protein synthesis will allow for pure-bred Hive offspring with no contamination from foreign biological material. We will birth live offspring with cellular level enhancements, perfect progeny without the need for external integration. Our race will flourish once more. We will be born, not integrated."

And the child growing in my womb would be the first of a new generation. Genetically altered. Integrated into a Hive creation even before he was born.

Tears burned the back of my eyelids, but I swallowed them down with rage. I didn't care if this baby was born with silver eyes, green skin and purple hair; it was mine, and I loved him already. Him? Her? It didn't matter. Mine. That was the only word that mattered. And these asshole aliens weren't getting their hands on my child.

When I remained silent, all three stepped back without turning around. "These are your quarters for the duration of your stay."

"You can't keep me here. My mate will come for me."

None responded to that. I tried another tact. "So the baby's Hive. Then what? You take my baby and I go home?"

"The breeding program was successful more quickly than expected."

"Breeding program?" I stared at him, eyes wide, mouth hanging open. I felt like a horse. *Bride* Program was one thing, but this? Hell no.

"Your future usefulness will be determined when you are delivered of the Hive infant."

"And until then?" I wondered, not willing to prod him for more information on that.

"Until then, you incubate Subject Zero-One."

"Incubate what?" Had they just assigned my baby a Hive designation? Named him? My stomach roiled, and I lifted my hand to cover my mouth as I gagged in panic. Their strange words, strange scientist-medical jargon had made me feel cold inside. But naming my baby? God, that made me sick. Scared. I backed away from them until my back hit the cold, sterile wall.

They turned as one and the door slid open. "We will return with nourishment and other garments to cover your body."

When I was alone, I stood there. Stunned. Amazed. Confused. Afraid.

Then I got mad. I went over every inch of the space, the first room.

"Incubate Subject Zero-One, my ass," I muttered, searching for some kind of communication device. Some kind of weapon. *Something.*

"Breeding program. My future usefulness. Ha!"

It took me awhile to realize there was no escape. I had a bedroom, not unlike Rezzer's on The Colony. I had to assume I was no longer *on* The Colony but some Hive place or planet or moon or whatever. All I knew was that I had a bedroom and a medical room all of my own. I was a breeding vessel for the first Hive baby, and they had no intention of letting me keep it, or even keeping me alive once it was born.

Unless it was to *breed.*

That was *not* happening.

I had two-hundred and sixty-four days to figure out how to get the hell out of here. I just had to hope that Rezzer took a whole hell of a lot less time finding me and getting me, and our baby, the fuck away from the triplets.

I hoped he came soon. And I hoped like hell his beast was ready to tear this place apart.

14

ezzer

IN THE BLINK OF AN EYE, I WAS NO LONGER IN THE CAVE WITH Kiel and the others. I was kneeling on the floor of a slick, bright interior and Caroline was dropping to her knees before me.

"Rezzer, oh my god!" she cried, wrapping her arms around me and knocking me on my ass.

I was stunned; no one took me out like that. But my body offered no resistance, recognizing her before my mind could catch up. Realizing I held no weapons in my hands—they must not have been allowed through the transport—I wrapped my arms around my mate and held her. Nothing else mattered. Only Caroline mattered.

Gods, she felt good. Soft and warm, her scent aroused and soothed my beast in equal measure. I held her as I lay on my back on the hard ground. Her mouth was on mine, kissing me ardently.

"Caroline. Where are we? The Hive."

"They're not here. At least not at the moment." She clung to me, shaking and frantic, touching me everywhere she could reach as if she needed to assure herself I was real.

She was shocked and trembling—and she smelled like them—the Hive. My beast roared from within, my hands roaming over every inch of her, burying their metallic scent as I assured myself she was unharmed. Her body was barely covered in a light gown, her bare bottom filling my hands as she submitted to my touch, somehow knowing I needed this as much as she did.

My cock thickened, pulsed between us. Every beast instinct roared to life, as if it had never been diminished by the Hive.

Fuck.

The Hive.

Regardless of how much I wanted my mate, I had to be vigilant, not voracious. I had no idea where the fuck we were. Whether or not we were safe.

Hells, we weren't safe. We were prisoners of the Hive.

"Mate," I breathed, looking around the space. From what I could see there was a bed and through an open door an exam room as if we were in a med unit. All was quiet. No beeps. Blips. Hive voices. No buzzing of invisible bars. "Are we alone?"

"I'm alone. These are the quarters they gave me."

"Quarters or med room?"

"Quarters. That lovely exam table is mine too. They believe I'm carrying a Hive baby."

My beast stilled. So did I. I sat up, gripped Caroline tightly. "Say that again."

Her dark eyes met mine. I only saw truth there. "They told me I'm carrying a Hive baby."

"That's a lie. Our baby, Caroline. Ours. The baby isn't Hive."

She shook her head slowly and clung to me, the desolation in her gaze more convincing than any words she could have spoken. Whatever she was about to tell me she believed to be true. And it was going to be bad. "The triplets call our baby Subject Zero-One. You are Subject Zero."

I was trying to process everything she said. "Triplets?" I asked.

"The three Hive guys. Two Prillon warriors and one creepy blue guy. He's the one in charge."

A Nexus unit. Fuck. Me. We were in even more trouble than I'd believed.

"Let's get off the floor and talk this through." I scooped her up and stood, looked around the room, peeked into the med room, grimaced. The space was foreboding, knowing the equipment, the table, were all for testing and assessing Caroline and our unborn child. I settled on the bed, the most calming spot in the two room quarters. Her legs wrapped around my waist and it felt good. Right. My beast calmed enough that I could think. "Now, tell me what you know."

I listened, horrified as she described her encounter with the Hive triplets, as she called them. She told me about the genetic splicing, the protein that was supposed to suppress my beast, the reason so few Atlans survived capture and Integration, and what they had planned for her. For us.

For the baby.

My beast lay quietly within, listening. Rage building. I held her, safe in my arms. It was the only thing keeping me under control.

"You're telling me they subdued my beast and tried to genetically alter my seed? That all of my cum was Hive contaminated? Designed to make our child more susceptible to Hive technology?"

She gave a slight shrug. "That's what they inferred."

Even though it had only been a few hours since I'd left her on The Colony, it felt as if so much had happened, but my beast snarled at the idea that our seed might be contaminated. "Our baby is not contaminated." I snarled out the words as I placed a hand between us, my palm against her flat belly. "What we did was not tainted by Hive."

She gave me a small smile, but her eyes welled with tears. "What if it is? What if there's something wrong with him?"

While I kept one hand on her belly, the other I lifted and cupped her jaw, swiped away her overflowing tears with my thumb. "Nothing that comes from you is bad. Our daughter, she will be perfect."

My heart all but thrummed out of my chest in equal parts rage, at having my mate saddened by such a sacred thing, and hope at what we'd made.

"Daughter?" she asked with a watery smile. "Did the doctor's wand tell us that?"

I shook my head. "I just know. She will have your sleek hair, black as night. And she will have me tied in knots, just like her mother."

She leaned in, put her head on my shoulder and cried. My beast growled, the rumble of it in my chest its own way to soothe her as I stroked my hand down her back, kissed the silky hair on top of her head.

She'd been through so much. Mated an alien, traveled across the galaxy. Fucked a beast out of dormancy and then into submission. Yes, she'd made my beast submit to her control, for without her near, he was wild. And now she was pregnant with a baby, a baby that the Hive wanted as their own.

"They will not have her," I said. "I am here because they want us both. I will protect you."

She lifted her head, stared at me with shiny eyes. "What

do you mean they want us both? I thought you're here to save me."

I gave her a slight smile. It wasn't filled with love or tenderness, but with the clear focus of my beast protecting what belonged to him. "I am here to save you. But I got here by Hive transport, just like you."

I leaned back, grabbed the transport beacon and plucked it from my shoulder. "Look familiar?"

Her mouth fell open as she stared at it. "That was what they used to transport me."

My beast growled.

"Did they hurt you?"

She glanced at her bare shoulder, and I saw no marks. "No, but I'd never transported awake before. It was really painful."

"Yes. While you had no idea what was happening, I did. The Hive were in the caves. They transported me as well. Not Kiel, not the others in our group. They wanted me specifically, and I knew you had been taken. I let them take me, Caroline. I had to get to you."

"What if you were wrong? What if they'd taken you somewhere else? What are we going to do?"

I heard the fear in her words. Scary aliens were going to take her. The thought of her being alone with the triplets even for an hour or two made me furious. I'd known about the Hive my entire life, fought them for years. She'd had two weeks of information about them—Rachel and Lindsey having told me that Earth knew almost nothing about the invasive enemy—and had absolutely zero contact. Until she was transported directly into the Hive den so they could steal her baby.

No. Fucking. Way.

My beast growled, and I started to grow.

"No!" she gasped. "Don't. Stop and think. Listen, Rezzer."

When she said my name, my beast calmed, focused. Settled. "Good. Why do they still want you? You had sex with me, put that Hive sperm of yours in me and made a baby. You're done now. It's my job to cook this kid and give it to them when it's done."

"Cook the kid?" I asked.

She rolled her eyes. "Earth slang. If you did your job—and they waved a wand over me and confirmed I'm still pregnant —then why do they need you?"

Yes, she raised an excellent question. Why did they need me? "They want my seed."

She nodded. "That's what they said. You did the job once, why not do it again? If they want a bunch of Hive babies, they need breeders. They plan on taking our baby, and impregnating me again. They said we were part of a breeding program."

I growled.

She stroked a hand over my hair and my beast all but leaned into the touch. "Their words, not mine."

"You're saying our job will be to fuck and make Hive babies?"

While I could do nothing but fuck her morning, noon and night and be content the rest of my life, I would not do it on command, and I would not do it for the Hive.

She shrugged. "But they think your beast is dormant. That whatever they did to you in those caves a few months ago is still intact."

"But you brought out the beast." I lifted her off my lap and stood, paced the small room. My beast growled to have Caroline back in my arms, but I needed space to think. The feel of her, her scent, the knowledge I didn't just hold her but our baby as well, clouded my mind.

I thought back to just before Caroline arrived. I'd had no sexual desire. No interest in a mate. It was as if the Hive had cut off my balls. But that was because I was an Atlan and subduing my beast was almost the same thing. I *could* have fucked, could have gotten a female pregnant with Hive contaminated seed. It wouldn't have been a true mating, but the contaminated seed could have been brought from my balls, perhaps even against my will.

She came up on her knees, the shine of excitement, of clarity in her eyes. "I brought out the beast, which was opposite of what the Hive wanted. But they don't know that. They still believe the beast is dead. You have to hide him, Rezz. Keep him under control until we can escape."

"What you ask is nearly impossible." The beast raged already. Pacing inside me like a wild thing desperate for vengeance. I was hot, sweating, so close to the edge of losing control that my body shivered hot, then cold, almost as if I had mating fever. "He will protect you, Caroline. I won't be able to stop him."

"I thought you never lose control." The challenge made my beast howl with both frustration and delight. By the gods, our mate was strong. I could not disappoint her.

"I will wait. But if they hurt you—"

"I know." Her smile was worth the vow I had just given her. She put her hand on her belly, the smile fading. "Do you really think this baby is Hive?"

I had no idea what that would entail, if the child would come out with a cyborg eye like Ryston, or completely contaminated. Silver flesh from head to toe? Would the babe have enhanced strength or intelligence? Or would the child look human? Atlan? The doctor's scans on The Colony hadn't discovered any anomalies, but, of course, he was scanning for a baby, not Hive contamination.

"I don't give a fuck what the baby is. It's ours. We made it. With love. As mates. There is nothing more pure than that. I love her, as is. And on The Colony, she will be accepted and understood. She will have a home. Family. Protection."

Tears filled her eyes again. "Oh, Rezzer."

I went to her then, wrapped my arms around her, kissed her. Gently. Tenderly.

"I want my cuffs back on you, mate." The weight of mine about my wrists had been the only thing that soothed the beast. She was mine and *nothing* was going to tear us apart now.

"Shhh. You're starting to growl. You have to hide your beast," she said.

It was going to be close to impossible. "As long as they don't hurt you. I will find a way to hold him back until the ReCon team arrives."

"We're being rescued?" she asked.

"Maxim was already working to track your transport when they took me. It is only a matter of time."

The door to the med room slid open, and I spun about, tucking Caroline behind me. Three Hive walked into the room, stood before me, ion pistols in hand.

"Subject Zero, we will separate you from your female breeder if you defy us."

My beast growled. Snarled. All but pressed against my skin to grow. I fought down the urge to change, to transform and rip their heads off. I fought the change because Caroline was right. They thought my beast dormant. No Hive would stand this close to an Atlan otherwise.

I offered a small nod, for I didn't dare speak.

"Female, sit on the table. We must perform further testing." The dark haired one issued the order and Caroline bit her lip, glancing from me to the blue creature who ignored the others, those black, fathomless eyes staring straight at me. I knew enough about the Hive, had heard whispers of the existence of the Nexus, the original Hive race. They were the control centers, the link between minds. Intelligent. Telepathic.

As strong as a beast.

I put my hands behind my back, gripped one wrist in a tight hold. Restraining myself.

Caroline gave me a quick glance and walked to the table, sat upon it, her feet dangling over the edge. She laid back; the seat reclined halfway.

"Do not touch her," I said, my voice unreasonably calm considering how I felt.

The trio looked to me.

The golden one spoke, the man once Prillon, now lost in the Hive mind. Their brains were connected. Where one spoke, they all thought. "Defy us and we will shoot the Atlan."

Caroline paled but didn't dare look at me. I studied the golden enemy, imagined how satisfying it would be to tear him in half. Decided I would kill him first.

"I see your beast has no concern for her beyond simple anger. Excellent." The blue Nexus unit spoke, and I chose not to respond.

"I will do as you say," Caroline replied, obviously trying to redirect their connected attentions away from me. "Leave him alone."

Beeping began. From the testing unit. From the wall. Caroline glanced at me, her eyes wide in panic as a strange moldable object was placed across her abdomen, down low, over her womb. It settled there, the interior of the jelly-like capsule flickering and sputtering with faint lights that coincided with new data streams appearing on the screens behind my mate's body.

"Protein A-T-Five-Seven not present. No Hive integration present. Genetic splice absent from the progeny. Recommend termination." A computerized voice came from the wall repeating the same thing over and over.

The testing showed what Caroline had guessed. She'd summoned the beast, healed me in a way I didn't fully understand, and my beast had taken over. Overridden or destroyed any Hive integration. My seed wasn't contaminated. The baby was beast and human. Not Hive. Not theirs.

Mine.

One Hive pressed a button on the wall and restraints came from the table, wrapping around my mate.

"What are you doing?" she cried.

"Fetus termination will commence immediately."

"Fetus termination?" Caroline asked, her voice shrill.

What? I growled, held my beast back. My mate was in danger. My baby was in danger.

"Subject Zero-One is not properly integrated. Therefore, the subject will be terminated, and you will be bred again."

"Rezzer!" Caroline cried, trying to wriggle free, but the restraints were too tight. The table shifted and moved automatically, her pinned legs lifting and spreading, her dress sliding up her thighs with the motion. A device lowered from the ceiling, a large needle affixed to the end.

Holy. Fuck. No.

"Rezzer!" she screamed.

My beast broke free.

15

<small>J</small>

Panic. Terror. Rage.

They all filled me up in a storm of emotion I couldn't control as the restraints twisted and pulled at my flesh. I fought, fought until my wrists were coated with blood, the slick wetness allowing me to pull harder.

Something popped in my hand. Broken bone? It hurt. Badly. But I didn't care. That fucking blue Hive bastard was not going to touch me or my baby.

"No fucking way!" I shouted aloud, to anyone who tried to get near me.

I pulled back and twisted my hand, trying to slide free as Rezzer's roar nearly deafened me. The Hive surrounding me turned completely away from me and the exam table, their attention on the real threat. The giant Atlan beast that wasn't supposed to be here. Yeah, full Atlan fucking beast. Rezzer had gone Hulk, towering over the trio, breathing hard, muscles pulsing and twitching, ready to kill.

A huge-ass beast that was supposed to be *suppressed*. Dormant. Weak.

"Surprise, you assholes." I whispered the words with glee as Rezzer rushed the Hive closest to him and tore the man in half. With his bare hands. As if he were a Ken doll and he'd yanked the plastic head off.

Gross.

I gagged, I couldn't help it. The smell of blood and death making it almost impossible to breathe. But I couldn't stop trying to get out of the damned restraints. I had to keep going. I had to fight as hard as Rezzer was fighting.

Rezzer lifted his huge fists and ripped the closest chair loose from where it had been attached to the ground. Bolts pinged against the wall.

The stupid Hive weren't expecting this. A beast. An Atlan so beyond rage that I wasn't even sure he would recognize me. His mate.

Nexus 4 turned away from Rezzer, his gaze roaming over me as he entered something into the screens on the wall. He looked confused, as if his plan had been so perfect there was no way it could go wrong. Until it did. Until the beast raged and destroyed.

"Reactivation protocol initiated." Nexus 4 was talking to someone, somewhere. I had no idea who or what, but he tilted his head just a bit, as if he was listening to something only he could hear. "Negative. Zero change." He glanced quickly at Rezzer, then turned back to the wall. "Increase strength of transmission signal."

A buzzing filled the room, the sound like a thousand mosquitos swarming us. Rezzer lifted his hands to his ears with a howl of agony and staggered to a stop, twisting side to side as if he were in great pain.

"Stop it!" I yelled at Nexus 4, but he and the remaining guard watched Rezzer, ignoring me completely.

Nexus 4 looked at his companion. "Shoot him with another dose of active microbots."

The half-silver Prillon lifted a strange gun from somewhere I couldn't see and pointed it at my mate.

He fired, hitting Rezzer with what looked like elephant sized tranquilizer darts filled with silver liquid. Rezzer screamed, the sound making my heart skip a beat as terror returned full force. I had to stop them. Had to fight harder. Fight or die.

They weren't taking me alive. They couldn't have my baby. And they couldn't have my mate.

With a cry of agony, I yanked my hand free of the restraint, sure that I'd broken more than one bone. But I didn't care. As the Nexus 4 entered data into the screen on the wall so quickly I couldn't see his fingers move beyond a strange blur, I reached over and freed my opposite hand. Leaning down, I grabbed the restraint on one ankle and pulled. The blue creature was so enthralled with watching Rezzer suffer that he wasn't even looking at me.

Until he did. Shit. Big blue hands covered mine, as if he didn't care if the other asshole were dismembered as long as he completed his mission: got Rezzer under control and terminated my baby. I shrieked in panic, because that so wasn't going to happen.

Rezzer's bellow shook my ribcage and Nexus 4 lifted his head as Rezzer lowered his hands from his head and straightened to his full height. The confused frown on the blue alien's face was the most beautiful thing I'd seen in my life. "Reactivation failure. The Atlan remains in beast mode."

He tilted his head with a strange tic of his brow. "Understood." His confusion cleared and he focused on me. "You will come with me." Nexus 4 wrapped both hands around the ankle strap and pulled, rending the thick restraint in half as easily as if he were pulling a piece of warm taffy into two parts.

But it wasn't taffy. It was steel. Or titanium. Something a lot harder than taffy.

Shit. He was strong. Much, much stronger than he looked.

Maybe even stronger than Rezzer's beast.

"No." I shoved at his hands when he reached for the restraint on my other ankle. "No!" I kicked at him with my free leg, but it was like kicking a brick wall, the pain of it reverberating up to my hip.

The Prillon Hive to my left screamed a challenge at my mate, whose answering growl was all the more frightening for its near silence.

Rezzer was in a fight for his life. And I was in a fight for mine. Mine and the little one I carried now.

The ankle restraint pulled in half and Nexus 4's hands wrapped around my thighs, pulling me toward him, off the table. His strength reminded me of Rezzer, but his touch…

I knew where he wanted to take me. Out the back door of the little exam room. Away from my mate. And once he had me away, he'd do unspeakable things. I was a *breeder*. While I wasn't Hive, or even had any Hive integrations, to them I was still a machine. A baby making machine. Nothing more.

I couldn't go with him.

I clung to the table, but my broken hand and lack of grip made it all too easy for Nexus 4 to pull harder, breaking my hold. "No."

I scrambled back, trying to get away, but his hands were nearly as large as Rezzer's. And strong. "Do not resist. I do not wish to harm you."

"Said every psychopath ever," I snarled at him.

That made him blink, the translucent, fish-like eyelid

creeping me out as Rezzer and the Prillon Hive rammed into each other, locked arms and smashed against the side wall so hard the floor rocked below me. "I am not a psychopath. It is illogical to hurt you or the Atlan. It does not serve our purpose."

Since he wasn't pulling on my legs at the moment, I tried to stall, looking around for a weapon. The light glinted off the needle-like thing they'd been about to prod me with. The thing they were going to use to kill my baby. "So, what is your purpose?"

"To create a perfect race free of contaminated integration. A pure race."

"What?"

His gaze drifted to where Rezzer and the Hive still fought. The sound of fists pummeling flesh was loud. I wondered why Rezzer hadn't just torn the guy in half already and been done with it like the other. "Kill him, Rezzer!" I yelled.

Nexus 4 shook his head. Calm. Too calm when he was facing down a beast. "Your mate lives because he must."

I turned and saw that Rezzer's chest was heaving. He was covered in blood, the killing rage in his eyes still there, but cold. Calculating. The Hive he faced did not advance, simply stared. And waited.

What the hell?

That was when I smelled it. Sickly sweet. My head started to spin, and I gasped, looking up to see a faint, misty presence of something being pumped into the air in the room. "Gas. They're poisoning us with gas."

I tried to yell, but already I had to fight just to form the words. The Hive didn't kill Rezzer because they wanted him alive. They wanted us both alive. For breeding.

Rezzer heard me and charged the Hive the same moment I reached for the needle, yanked it from its metallic arm and jammed it into the Nexus's cheek. He calmly lifted his hands to his face to remove the metal, and I rolled backward, off the table, away from him. Not the response I wanted, wishing he'd at a minimum shriek in pain, but it had bought me some time.

I was running the second my feet hit the floor, trying not to breathe in the gas. Even if Nexus 4 and the Hive were knocked out, wherever we were, outside the room we were still surrounded by enemies. They were not. If we fell now, we'd wake up exactly where we'd been before. Prisoners. Helpless. And I had a sinking feeling my baby would be gone.

Rezzer threw the Hive halfway across the room, his body slamming through the thick walls before sliding to the ground, stunned. He wasn't dead, but he wasn't moving too quickly either.

I clung to the wall as far away from the Hive Rezzer fought as I could get and moved toward my mate. Nexus 4 just watched me with an expression devoid of emotion. He knew the gas was going to take us all out. Knew, and waited like a spider in the middle of his giant, nasty web.

I fucking hated spiders.

"Rezzer, they're pumping knock-out gas into the room. We have to get out of here."

The beast turned to me, his green eyes practically glowing with battle lust, but he was gentle as he pulled me to his chest, picked me up and swung me around onto his back.

"Hold. Tight," his beast ordered as he turned his attention to the wall in front of him. I wrapped my legs around his beast-sized hips the best I could, my arms around his neck and plastered myself to his back to protect him as he raised both fists over his head and roared. Nexus 4 might shoot at Rezzer, but he wouldn't shoot me, his prize breeder and future Hive baby-maker. Rezzer might be able to survive a blast from the space weapons, but me? I was human. If Nexus

4 shot me, I had no idea how much damage would be done. Whether or not I would survive.

Apparently, Nexus 4 didn't either. Our gazes met and held as Rezzer struck twice more against the wall in rapid succession. The blue creature looked almost…sad.

The wall crumbled on Rezzer's third strike, and he kicked his way through. The blast of fresh air hit me like an icy breeze, and I sucked in deep, gulping breaths trying to clear my head and my lungs. We were so out of here.

Darting low, Rezzer ducked through the opening and out into a long gray corridor.

But I was slipping. My bloody, broken hand shooting agony through me every time I tried to tighten my hold.

"Rezz."

In seconds I was in his arms, cradled protectively against his chest as he raced down the corridor. Thank god. My hand was killing me and shock was making me tremble. I was falling apart at the seams. I'd held on for this long, but I wasn't a warrior or a Warlord. I wasn't used to such adrenaline inducing situations. Of life and death. "Do you know where you're going?" I asked.

"Maxim. Transport."

Two words. Music to my ears. These big beasts communicated just fine. "Thank god. The cavalry is coming?"

"ReCon."

Whatever that meant, although I realized he might not have understood what the cavalry meant. It wasn't like they had horses in space, at least that I knew of. I trusted him to take care of me. I didn't have any other choice. Nor did I want one.

We rounded a corner and the sounds of shouting and some kind of blasting reached us. I looked up, saw Rezzer grin. "ReCon. Here." He picked up his pace, running faster than I would have believed a beast his size could move. Two turns later, I was face-to-face with Lieutenant Denzel in full battle armor.

He took one look at us with his silver eyes through the clear mask of his helmet and motioned for the big beast to move behind him.

It should have been laughable, a human protecting a beast, but Rezzer went around him with a nod of thanks and Denzel lifted his space rifle to cover our retreat.

"You all right?" Denzel yelled, and I realized he wasn't talking to Rezz, he was talking to me.

"Yeah, I'm good." And I was. Rezzer had me in his arms. The baby was safe. Nothing else mattered.

Denzel gave a nod and the ReCon team from The Colony, all human, swarmed around us like bees. "Transport is two corridors up on the right, Warlord."

Rezzer grunted his thanks and took off running. The ReCon team fell in behind us like water, protecting our retreat.

Shots were fired. The men yelled. I couldn't keep track of what was happening and couldn't see beyond the massive wall of Rezzer's chest. But when we all raced up onto the transport platform, I welcomed the electric pull, the wrenching pain this time. The twisting agony.

It meant we were going home.

16

"I STILL THINK YOU NEED TO GO TO THE DOCTOR TO BE monitored." Rezzer's deep voice carried over the splash of water, and I sighed, putting the back of my head under the hot water and letting the heat stream over me like a caress.

I was standing in the shower tube, rinsing off the time with the Hive. Rezzer and his beast had saved me from the creepy triplets. But still, being held as a breeder to make Hive babies? Yeah, that was something I wanted to forget.

We'd all been seen by the medical staff. I'd had my hand healed by a thing called a ReGen wand. It was an incredible piece of technology. The baby was fine. I was fine. The others were fine, too. Only minor injuries to the ReCon group, and the wand had healed them, too.

But now, Rezzer worried I would need constant medical monitoring to make sure that Nexus 4's threats about our baby didn't magically appear. Testing every day. Hell, he was so freaked, he had walked me to Doctor Surnen at least three times since we'd been back. If he had his way, the doctor would just move in with us. Not happening.

This baby was fine. Rezzer was fine. His beast had won, beaten the stupid genetic splicing. The doctor said Rezzer's natural physiology destabilized the proteins created by Hive biosynthetics. Basically, Rezzer's body chemistry was a hostile environment for Hive technology. And when an Atlan went beast, it was even worse.

So this baby? Our baby? Perfect. Healthy. But everyone was concerned with what the Hive had said to me. Pure born? Breeding programs? Rachel especially had been fascinated by the concept that Nexus 4 said integrating other species into the Hive was contamination.

Nexus 4 had wanted my baby to save his race. To be a bridge between the synthetic, created Hive and a new generation of babies born to them. The thought was both frightening and unbearably sad.

I slid my soapy hand over my belly, wondering what had happened to their people. How they'd gotten to this place, where they could no longer survive on their own. Have their own children...

"What's wrong?" Rezzer yanked open the door, looking down at me with a fierce scowl, yet a hint of fear in his green eyes. The spray coated his uniform with drops of water, then seeped into the black material.

I rolled my eyes. Damned possessive mate.

But he was ridiculously concerned for me—and rightly so —and I had to indulge him. While he was the Atlan version of the Incredible Hulk, he had a tender heart. Besides, he did just say he *wanted* me to go to the doctor, but he wasn't tossing me over his shoulder and forcing me there.

And so I soothed my big mate. "Nothing is wrong. The baby is fine. I'm fine." I lifted my hand, curled my fingers into a fist so he could see that was all better. "Doctor Surnen has run every test he has. The baby is fine. Healthy. You were there. I was just thinking about how much I want this baby, Hive parts or not."

He softened then, the hard lines of his body easing. "Our child will be loved, Caroline. Protected. Nothing will ever hurt either of you again."

And that was the crux of my problem. The reason I was trembling. Worried. "I just worry they will keep coming after us. Try to take me again. Take the baby."

He reached in, touched my chin, forced me to lift my eyes to his. "The Hive know their little experiment didn't work. They have the data in their computers, witnessed my beast defeating their genetic splicing as well as the attack of microtech and activation frequencies in that lab. I am beyond their reach now, because of you. You made my beast stronger than ever. Their experiment failed."

"But what will keep them from trying again?" I shivered, even under the warm spray.

He dropped his hand. "They most likely will try again, but not with me. I am a failure to them, and they will try to find a weaker test subject."

"A weak beast?" I couldn't imagine such a thing.

He studied me, his eyes dark. Serious. "The ruling Senate of Atlan has been notified of all that occurred. They will be vigilant. Even now, word is being spread throughout the Fleet. Within a few days, every elected Atlan commander will know what is at stake when they face the Hive. It is all we can do."

"But why an Atlan? Why not a Prillon or one of the other races? If you guys are almost impossible to integrate in the first place, why did they choose a beast for this experiment?" I didn't like the idea of the Hive using some other Coalition male for their breeding program, but the analyst in me was crunching numbers, thinking about the odds. "You know that you probably aren't their only test subject, right? It doesn't make sense that you'd be the only one."

God, I hated even saying it out loud, but it had to be said. The governor and the Fleet, the scientists or whoever was in charge of that kind of thing, needed to be thinking straight. "This isn't the end, Rezz."

"It is for us. I fought my war, mate. I gave my life and my body. And now, do you know what I want?" His eyes were dark, but not with concern. No. I'd seen this look too many times to mistake it for anything but what it was. Lust. Love. A combustible mix of the two that made my knees weak and my heart race. We'd survived. Our baby was well. That was all that mattered now.

"No. But I know what I want," I teased.

He ripped his shirt off, dropped his thigh holster to the floor, then stripped bare at a record pace. His mood shifted faster than a teenaged girl. "Tell me."

I eyed him. Every big, hard, delectable inch. My mouth watered and even under the hot spray, I knew my pussy was wet. My nipples pebbled, and my already high-revving libido kicked into overdrive. Now that we were free of the Hive, for good this time, I just wanted Rezzer. Nothing else. "You. I want you."

We'd been in danger I wouldn't have been able to fathom on Earth. When it came to life and death, we'd made it out alive; I just wanted to validate that. To feel, knowing that we'd survived. That we were whole. To prove my love for Rezzer.

He pushed forward, and I held him off with a hand on his chest. "You can't think to get in here with me," I said with a laugh. "You won't fit."

The shower tube was big enough to fit Rezzer, but not both of us. It wasn't a two-person marble shower with six showerheads like they had on Earth. This was utilitarian. Hmm. Maybe this was something to talk about with the other ladies from Earth. Getting them made. Surely, they'd like some shower nookie.

When Rezzer pushed a button and the water shut off, he grabbed a large towel, tugged my hand so I stepped out of the narrow space and wrapped me in it. He dried me with gentle hands, then rubbed the excess water from my long hair.

"No," he replied. "We need lots of space for what I plan to do to you."

"Plan? You've planned it?"

"Mate, I think about what I'm going to do to you about twenty times an hour. It's a wonder I get anything else done."

I giggled then. This was a completely new side to Rezzer. Gone was the bossiness.

"On the bed, mate. Knees bent, legs spread. I want to see that perfect pussy."

Well, not gone completely. But this bossiness I didn't mind.

I slipped from the towel and walked into the bedroom, a gentle swat to my butt getting me to move faster. Sliding across the soft blanket, I laid down, then rolled onto my back. Crossing his arms over his broad chest, he watched. Eyebrow arching, he waited. Bending my knees, I planted my feet on the edge of the bed, spread wide.

Yeah, this totally worked for me. Doing what my mate said. Baring myself. Exposing not only my body, but my heart as well. The way Rezzer's eyes went dark, like a forest at dusk, I knew he liked what he saw. And while he might be the one in charge, I could certainly exert my own power.

I slipped a finger between my lips, sucked on the tip, then slid it down my chest and to my nipple, circling it about. His eyes followed my action, and his gaze narrowed. From there,

I moved it down my body and between my legs, circling once again, this time my clit.

"Mate," Rezzer warned. My eyes were heavy-lidded, and I saw the beast coming to the surface.

He took a deep breath, and I knew he was trying to control the beast. Inwardly, I smiled.

He stalked around the bed, lay down on it so his head was on the pillows. I had to look awkwardly over my shoulder to look at him. I frowned.

"Up, mate."

I rolled and came up onto my knees.

He looked to me, crooked a finger. "Change of plans."

"Oh?" I asked innocently.

"Don't give me that, mate. I know what you're trying to do."

"Oh?"

His beast gave a small growl. "I'm in control this time. Over you. And my beast. I won't take you rough. Or wild."

"Okay," I replied, feeling my pussy gush with my arousal. God, being pregnant made me so needy. And I loved it. By the way Rezzer's cock bobbed and pulsed against his belly, he loved it too.

"Climb up here and sit on my face."

"Um…what?"

He grinned then. "Ah, something you haven't done. Get up here, female. I want a taste of that pussy."

My inner walls clenched at the idea. Every time he'd gone down on me before, I'd been flat on my back, my legs tossed over his shoulders. He'd been very thorough about it. But this? I swallowed, looking my fill of him. Saw the determination in his eyes. The drop of pre-cum on the tip of his cock.

Yeah, I wanted a taste of him, too.

Instead of obeying, I put my hand on the bed, leaned down and licked off the salty fluid.

The rumble that escaped his chest and reverberated off the room's walls was all beast.

With a gasp, his hands grabbed me, and he lifted me up so I was hovering over him. I looked down at him, past my breasts and saw his eyes. At first, they held mine, then took in my pussy. No doubt he could see I was swollen and wet for him.

Slowly, he lowered me down, giving me time to adjust my legs so that I was kneeling on either side of his head. But once I was settled, he took hold of my butt and pulled me to him so I was sitting directly on his face.

I gripped the plain metal frame of the headboard and held on for dear life. He was ruthless, merciless, with his tongue, with his lips. Sucking, laving, flicking. All kinds of verbs that described his incredible oral skills.

"Holy shit," I breathed, my eyes falling closed, my chin tipping up to the ceiling.

It felt so good. My clit was seemingly always hard now, primed, and I was ready to come. And with his tongue on me, I came quickly.

"Rezzer!"

The pleasure washed through me, my thighs clenching about his ears, my pussy dripping all over his face. He didn't stop, only growled with obvious male satisfaction at making me come so damned easily.

I tried to catch my breath, but he wouldn't relent, only pushed me to the brink with another swift, fierce orgasm.

"It's too much. Oh!"

Yeah, it wasn't too much, especially since he made me come a third time before he pushed me up a few inches.

"I love your taste. I could spend hours here."

"Rezzer, I'm too sensitive." I was sweating, and I was panting. My toes tingled.

"Good."

Good?

He shifted one hand so his fingers slipped over my slick folds, then slid inside.

I arched my back at the feel of something inside me. Even two of his fingers didn't match the girth of his cock. But his cock didn't have the same dexterity, for he curled those digits over my g-spot, and I was ready to come again.

Just. Like. That.

"Rezzer!" I cried again.

"That's my mate. Yes. Good girl."

Only when I came down from that bout of pleasure did he flip me onto my back and shifted to loom over me, one of his tree-trunk sized legs between mine. The feel of his thigh against my pussy made me gasp again.

Yeah, sensitive.

"I can't take anymore." The cool sheets felt good on my back. I was ready to sleep, content and blissfully sated.

"You can and you will. You think I'm done with you?"

I blinked my eyes open and saw he was serious.

"Do I have to link your cuffs together?"

That question brought back the first time we fucked. I'd just arrived and I'd been surprised by the cuffs—didn't know the meaning of them—and found them erotic. I liked being restrained and at Rezzer's mercy. But now, knowing the value of the cuffs prompted me to the extent of our bond.

I smiled softly up at my mate. I lifted a hand, cupped his jaw, felt the soft rasp of his whiskers. "You don't have to do anything to keep me. You are my mate. The perfect match out of all the males in the entire universe. You are mine, Rezzer. I am bound to you by invisible bonds. Bonds that no one can break."

A slow smile crept across his face. "Yes, mate. I see you understand. The cuffs are an outward sign of our love, our devotion. Our permanent connection. But this, having you beneath me. Having you trust me so implicitly with your body, with your *soul*, it's more than either I, or my beast, can express."

Whoa. That was heavy. Deep and so wonderfully perfect.

Tears filled my eyes even as I smiled.

"You are upset?" he asked, wild concern in his gaze, although I couldn't see much of it through my tears.

I shook my head, felt a tear slide down my temple and into my hair. "The opposite. So happy."

His big hands cupped my face, thumbs wiping the tears away.

"I was going to distance myself. Go to outer space. Have a match, but not care. I was prepared to be indifferent."

"Mate," he growled.

"Shh," I soothed. I loved the hard press of him into the mattress, the thick line of his cock against my inner thigh. "I wasn't prepared for you."

Cocking his head to the side, he studied me, then lowered his head. Kissed me. Either the beast was subdued or had learned to be gentle. Tender.

Our tongues met, played. While it was just as hot as every other kiss, it was different. Perfect.

This wasn't just fucking. For the first time in my life, I knew this for what it was. Making love.

With my big cyborg beast.

I lifted my hips, although he didn't give me much room to move, but he felt my shift.

Lifting his head, he murmured against my mouth. "Eager for more?"

I nodded.

"Even after all those orgasms?"

I whimpered. Ready for more. While I was still needy, still sensitive, our little chat had taken the edge off.

"Such a greedy mate," he said, shifting to the side so he could slide his hand between us, over me. Featherlight, I wasn't sure if he was really touching me or if it was my imagination. "Don't worry. I'll always see to your needs."

I reached around and grabbed his perfect muscular ass. Pulled him toward me. "I *need* you inside me."

He growled. There was my beast.

He shifted, settled between my parted thighs, slid right into me.

I gasped at the thick feel of him. The stretching. The filling.

"Yes," I hissed, loving every inch of him.

He came up onto his forearms, kept his weight off of me, but I felt every long, hard inch of him. We were connected. Joined.

One.

"Mate," I said. "Mine."

The beast growled as Rezzer began to move. Slowly, almost leisurely, he took me, stroking my hair back from my face, his eyes meeting mine. Holding me pinned that way as well.

"Mine," he replied.

But his slow pace wasn't enough. I wanted more. I wanted the beast to fuck me too. "More," I said, lifting my hips up to meet every stroke.

He stilled. I growled. Yes, growled. The jerk was teasing me.

"Rezzer, I need more."

"Tell me exactly what you need."

I sucked in a breath. "Hard. Deep. Mark me."

He held himself still for one more second before he

grabbed my wrists by the cuffs, lifted them over my head, pinned them there with one of his. Cuff to cuff.

His other hand hooked behind a knee, pushed back, opened me wide for him.

"As my mate wishes."

He fucked me then. Just as I wanted. Needed.

"Yes," I breathed.

The wet sound of fucking filled the air. The musky scent of it swirled around us. The heat on my skin melded with his.

His hips slapped against my ass, pushing me to climax this time. There was no coaxing. This was an all out attack, and I couldn't defend myself. Nor did I want to.

I cried his name, over and over, each time he bottomed out.

I felt him thicken, swell within me and shout my name. Surely, those in the hallway heard. But definitely did when my scream of pleasure mixed with it.

I didn't care. I wanted the whole world—universe—to know Rezzer was mine. That the baby inside me was made because of our perfect connection. Our match.

Rezzer collapsed, falling to the bed beside me, one hand slung over my waist, pulling me with him. He didn't pull out. I felt his seed, thick and potent, slip from me, but he seemed content to remain within.

I wasn't going to complain. I had everything I ever wanted, but never knew existed.

I was the luckiest woman in the universe.

EPILOGUE

I was sprawled across Rezzer's chest, my head tucked beneath his chin. I was so tired I fought to keep my eyelids open as Rezzer's steady heartbeat lulled me into perfect contentment. I'd heard babies turned parents into zombies, never getting enough sleep, but I hadn't realized how bad it was until now. Rachel and Kristin were helping out as much as they could, but they had their own little ones to manage.

Surprisingly, it had been the older women, the grandmothers, Lindsey's mother Carla from Earth and Lady Ryall, the Prillon warrior Ryston's mother, Rachel's mother-in-law, who had kept me sane.

Little RJ stirred on his father's chest, made a funny little grunting sound. I smiled, looking down at our sleeping son. Rezzer, Jr.

He was swaddled in the softest of fabrics, his head covered in a tiny cap, hiding the fact that he was completely bald. There was a hint of dark fuzz, but nothing else. His eyes were dark brown, like mine, but his face? He was Atlan, the baby beast so much like his father already that it hurt to look at him.

My mate was big enough that we could all lay across him as we napped, Rezzer and I both trying to catch some shut eye as our babies slept.

Yes, babies.

Rezzer, Jr.—better known as RJ—and his little sister. Littler by five minutes. His twin. Caroline, Junior. Yes, it was crazy having a daughter named the same as me, but Rezzer wasn't from Earth and insisted if our boy child was named after him, our daughter would have my name. And since he called me Caroline, our little black-haired beauty was CJ.

RJ and CJ. Corny, sappy and so perfect. They'd had half the base here to meet them already. Even Warlord Braun, the big brute, had brought them little gifts, held them in his gigantic hands and sung to them with the sweetest, deepest voice I'd ever heard. I'd started crying, blamed it on hormones, and sent a prayer up to whatever gods would listen to send the Atlan his own mate soon.

Our revolving door was just the beginning. From what I'd heard from Rachel, the governors of the other bases would arrive soon for a feast where all the children would be celebrated as the miracles they were.

"Sleep, mate," Rezzer said, his voice low and rumbly. RJ was on top of his big chest and CJ was asleep in the crook of his arm. She reminded me of a tiny peanut, a pound smaller than her brother, she had a head full of shocking black hair and Rezzer's green eyes.

When we'd been held by the Hive, I'd dreamed of this. Being in bed with Rezzer and our baby. I'd gotten it. And a bonus.

"I'm just amazed by them." I couldn't stop staring at them.

Their perfect little hands. Amazing little faces. We'd done that. Me and Rezzer. Together.

I felt his laugh through his chest. "Not as amazed as Doctor Surnen. Atlans do not give birth to twins."

"Well, I'm not an Atlan." Doctor Surnen hadn't even bothered to look for a second baby. And like a typical Atlan, little RJ had kept his sister hidden and protected behind his larger body. Rezzer insisted it was his son's beast, aware, even in the womb, of his role as protector. I didn't argue. Until the little guy was old enough to talk, I'd be happy to let his proud papa keep his fantasies.

I had no idea how the doctor had missed *her*. A second heartbeat. Two babies. I'd been absolutely enormous—like a beached whale—when I finally went into labor. But everyone, including me, thought I was just having a huge beast baby. But no. Only when I'd delivered RJ and then decided I had the desperate need to push again, did we discover I'd been incubating two beautiful half-human/half Atlan babies. Not a hint of Hive in them.

The look on the doctor's face had been priceless, but I'd never forget Rezzer's. Especially when he'd held each newborn in his arms. In awe. His beast, for once, completely tame.

"You have very potent swimmers."

Rezzer was still for a minute, mentally processing my Earth slang. "We should make more."

It was my turn to still. "You push something out your penis—no, two somethings—and then we'll talk," I grumbled. It had been a week since I delivered, and—as Kristin promised—the ReGen Pods were amazing. My body was almost back to normal. But twins were exhausting, and I wasn't quite ready to get it on with my sexy mate. I knew my desire would return, but for now, I was content being in awe of our little ones.

He laughed again, then kissed the top of my head. "A fair statement. I will suggest it again. Later."

"Later," I agreed, knowing he would probably get his way. I smiled and turned my head to kiss him on the chest as his arm tightened around me with the strength and protection I'd not only grown to rely on, but to love. "I love you, Rezzer."

"You are my heart, mate. It does not beat without you."

Love? Such a tame word for what he meant to me. I settled, admiring the mating cuffs securely back on my wrists where they belonged. When I left for work with the acquisitions team, or he left to do his security runs, I had to take them off. But he refused to remove his. They'd never left his wrists, not once. And I knew they never would.

"Sleep now, Caroline. The babies will be reminding us who is in charge very soon."

He was right. While Rezzer liked to be the one in control, it had been two tiny infants who had ripped that away from him. And as I fell asleep, I smiled, knowing he was perfectly happy to let them have their way.

His beast, too.

A SPECIAL THANK YOU TO MY READERS...

Want more? I've got **hidden** bonus content on my web
site *exclusively* for those on my mailing list.

If you are already on my email list, you don't need to do a thing!
Simply scroll to the bottom of my newsletter emails and click on
the **super-secret** link.

Not a member? What are you waiting for? In addition to ALL of my
bonus content (great new stuff will be added regularly) you will be
the first to hear about my newest release the second it hits the stores
—AND you will get a free book as a special welcome gift.

Sign up now! http://freescifiromance.com

FIND YOUR INTERSTELLAR MATCH!

YOUR mate is out there. Take the test today and discover your perfect match. Are you ready for a sexy alien mate (or two)?

VOLUNTEER NOW!

interstellarbridesprogram.com

DO YOU LOVE AUDIOBOOKS?

Grace Goodwin's books are now available as
audiobooks…everywhere.

LET'S TALK SPOILER ROOM!

Interested in joining my **Sci-Fi Squad**? Meet new like-minded sci-fi romance fanatics and chat with Grace! Get excerpts, cover reveals and sneak peeks before anyone else. Be part of a private Facebook group that shares pictures and fun news! Join here:

https://www.facebook.com/groups/scifisquad/

***

Want to talk about Grace Goodwin books with others? Join the **SPOILER ROOM** and spoil away! Your GG BFFs are waiting! (And so is Grace)

Join here:

https://www.facebook.com/groups/ggspoilerroom/

GET A FREE BOOK!

Join my mailing list to be the first to know of new releases, free books, special prices and other author giveaways.

http://freescifiromance.com

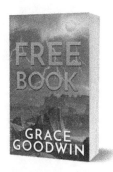

ALSO BY GRACE GOODWIN

Cyborg Fever

Rogue Cyborg

Cyborg's Secret Baby

Interstellar Brides® Program: The Virgins

The Alien's Mate

Claiming His Virgin

His Virgin Mate

His Virgin Bride

Interstellar Brides® Program: Ascension Saga

Ascension Saga, book 1

Ascension Saga, book 2

Ascension Saga, book 3

Trinity: Ascension Saga - Volume 1

Ascension Saga, book 4

Ascension Saga, book 5

Ascension Saga, book 6

Faith: Ascension Saga - Volume 2

Ascension Saga, book 7

Ascension Saga, book 8

Ascension Saga, book 9

Destiny: Ascension Saga - Volume 3

Other Books

Their Conquered Bride

Wild Wolf Claiming: A Howl's Romance

ABOUT GRACE

Grace Goodwin is a *USA Today* and international bestselling author of Sci-Fi & Paranormal romance. Grace believes all women should be treated like royalty, in the bedroom and out of it, and writes love stories where men know how to make their women feel pampered, protected and very well taken care of. Grace hates the snow, loves the mountains (yes, that's a problem) and wishes she could simply download the stories out of her head instead of being forced to type them out. Grace lives in the western US and is a full-time writer, an avid reader and an admitted caffeine addict. She is active on Facebook and loves to chat with readers and fellow sci-fi fanatics.

All of Grace's books can be read as sexy, stand-alone adventures. But be careful, she likes her heroes hot and her love scenes hotter. You have been warned...

www.gracegoodwin.com
gracegoodwinauthor@gmail.com

CPSIA information can be obtained
at www.ICGtesting.com
Printed in the USA
BVHW041520201120
593806BV00012B/1203